FROM THE NANCY DREW FILES

THE CASE: Find out who's spreading terror through the offices of Flash, the hottest new teen magazine in the country.

CONTACT: Yvonne Verdi, publisher of Flash. Her life is being threatened, but an investigation could ruin her career.

SUSPECTS: Mick Swanson, the magazine's art director. He's creative and brilliant, but his temper is sheer murder.

Sondra Swanson, Mick's sister. She's fiercely loyal to her brother. Is she lying to Nancy to cover up for him?

David Bowers, the magazine's editor in chief and Yvonne's new boyfriend. Is he after her job—or her life?

COMPLICATIONS: Ned is getting sick of Nancy's sleuthing, and Sondra Swanson may be just the cure he needs. But Nancy has more to worry about than losing her boyfriend—she's losing her job. If she's off the case, how can she stop a murderer?

Books in THE NANCY DREW FILES™ Series

Available from ARCHWAY paperbacks

THE
NANCY DREW
FILES™ CASE • 4

SMILE AND
SAY MURDER

Carolyn Keene

AN ARCHWAY PAPERBACK
Published by POCKET BOOKS • NEW YORK

AN ARCHWAY PAPERBACK *Original*

An Archway Paperback published by
POCKET BOOKS, a division of Simon & Schuster, Inc.
1230 Avenue of the Americas, New York, N.Y. 10020

ISBN: 0-671-62557-8

First Archway Paperback printing October, 1986

10 9 8 7 6 5 4 3 2 1

NANCY DREW, AN ARCHWAY PAPERBACK and colophon
are registered trademarks of Simon & Schuster, Inc.

THE NANCY DREW FILES is a trademark
of Simon & Schuster, Inc.

Printed in the U.S.A.

IL 7+

SMILE AND SAY MURDER

Chapter

One

NANCY DREW SANK back into the cushioned seat of the commuter train that traveled between River Heights and Chicago and pulled a glossy new magazine out of her shoulder bag. The star of the hottest new TV show smiled sexily at her from the cover. Above his head, in bold pink letters, was the word *FLASH*.

Nancy opened the magazine and skimmed articles about a sixteen-year-old ballet star in Atlanta, a fashion show fundraiser at glitzy Hollywood High School, and a college freshman in Nevada who'd discovered a cure for acne. Without a doubt, Nancy told herself, *Flash* magazine is a winner. No wonder kids all over the country were snatching it up the second it was out on the newsstands.

Nancy had been meaning to pick up a copy

1

for a few weeks, ever since one of her best friends, Bess Marvin, had started raving about it. At the moment, though, Nancy wasn't just trying to pass a boring ride from the suburbs into the city. She was doing research on a new mystery, a mystery that was bound to take her on a flashy adventure.

Urgent—that was how *Flash* magazine's publisher and co-owner had described the situation to Nancy on the phone the other night. And it wasn't slipping sales figures that had Yvonne Verdi worried. Someone had been sending her threatening letters—ugly ones—and she was scared stiff.

Nancy closed the magazine and stared out the train window as suburb melted into suburb. It would have been nicer to drive into the city, but she knew finding a parking space would be completely hopeless. If I decide to take the case, she told herself, I'd better get used to being a commuter. I'm going to have to make the trip every morning, and Dad is against the idea of my driving in all that city traffic.

Nancy's mother had died when Nancy was just a child. So for most of her eighteen years it had been just her and her father, Carson Drew, a highly successful lawyer. Nancy figured she and her father had to take care of each other— with a little help from Hannah Gruen, the Drews' loving housekeeper. Nancy hated to hassle with her father. She figured the best way to avoid that was to leave her blue Mustang at home for the time being.

Nancy's thoughts returned to the new case. It made her heart pound with excitement. Even if the letters turned out to be just some creep's idea of a prank, she'd get a chance to see the inner workings of the number-one teen magazine. Of course, there was always the chance that the threats were serious.

Either way, Nancy felt sure she was prepared. With dozens of difficult and successfully solved mysteries behind her, she'd seen through the most carefully constructed criminal plots, and she was ready to do it all over again.

Nancy crossed her slim, shapely legs and ran her hand through her reddish blond, shoulder-length hair. Starting a case was like running a cross-country race. You knew that once the gun went off, you had to reach the finish line before the other guy, but you weren't quite sure how you were going to get there. That meant you had to be especially alert and observant, or you'd end up following a lot of dead-end trails.

Nancy's keen blue eyes gazed resolutely at the handsome face of the star on the *Flash* cover. "Whatever secrets you're trying to hide," she said to the magazine, "they're not going to stay secret for long!"

As the train pulled into Chicago's main terminal, Nancy stood up, straightened her blue angora sweater dress, and grabbed her gray jacket and shoulder bag from the seat. She hurried outside and found a taxi. Twenty minutes later, she was standing in front of the *Flash* offices on Michigan Avenue. Here goes, she thought. She took a deep breath and stepped into the building.

Nancy waited for the elevator with a businessman and two bicycle messengers. When the doors opened, two casually dressed women walked out.

"Really, Yvonne is pushing me too far," one of the women was saying. "I don't care if she *is* the co-owner of the magazine. If she makes one more comment to me about 'proper office clothes' I'm going to . . . well, I don't know what, but I'm going to do something."

"She's definitely annoying," the other woman replied. "But don't take it personally. She bugs everyone, not just you."

Nancy listened with interest. Clearly, the women were discussing *Flash*'s co-owner—and they weren't too fond of her.

Nancy stepped into the elevator and pressed the button for the sixteenth floor. The doors opened onto *Flash*'s reception area, a large, spacious room decorated in a style Nancy liked to call super-tech. Sparse but tasteful, and very, very expensive. Huge glass windows gave a perfect view of Lake Michigan, and a brightly colored painting hung on one wall. Two long hallways, one pale blue, the other cream, led in opposite directions. Through an open door on the right, Nancy noticed six or seven brand-new computers. There was a computer at the reception desk, too. Obviously *Flash* wasn't hurting for fancy new equipment.

Nancy walked up to the young man behind

the reception desk. He was playing a game of Clone Wars on the computer. "Hold on," he said without looking up. "I just have to get this last clone." He played intently for another thirty seconds. "Got him!" he cried. "Okay, who are you and what can I do for you?" he asked, finally paying attention to Nancy.

"My name's Nancy Drew. I'm here to see Yvonne Verdi."

"Ah, the queen clone herself. If only it were as easy as a game." The receptionist sighed. "She's expecting you. Her office is down that hall and on the left." He pointed to the cream-colored hallway.

Nancy smiled and headed in the direction he had pointed, filing away another bit of information. Already she had the feeling that Yvonne wasn't too well liked around *Flash*.

Nancy found Yvonne's office and knocked. "Come in," called a voice. Nancy opened the door and stepped in. "Nancy Drew," the woman behind the desk said as she got to her feet. "Welcome to *Flash!*" She extended her hand to Nancy.

At five feet eight inches, Yvonne Verdi was only slightly taller than Nancy, but her imposing presence made Nancy feel almost small. She was one of those hot young business people who obviously had it all. Nancy decided she couldn't be more than twenty-seven years old. In her stylish skirt and jacket, with her black hair swept into a French knot and her dark eyes flashing, she didn't seem like a woman anyone would want to mess around with. The writer of the letters was either very tough or very crazy to be threatening Yvonne Verdi.

"Glad to meet you, Ms. Verdi," Nancy said, shaking the publisher's hand.

"Call me Yvonne," the publisher replied. "We go by first names around here. Please, have a seat." She gestured to a cushy black leather couch, and Nancy sank comfortably into it. "Okay, let's get down to business." Yvonne pulled two envelopes out of a desk drawer and sat down herself. "These are the reasons I called you here today."

Nancy smiled sympathetically. "Threatening letters can be very upsetting," she said, "but they're not always serious. Sometimes the writers only mean to scare their—"

"Oh, but these particular letters *are* serious," Yvonne cut in. "Nancy, someone's trying to kill me!"

Nancy studied Yvonne's face. It was hard to tell what she was feeling. "Why are you so sure of that?" she asked.

"Because I know who's trying to do it!" Yvonne threw the letters down on her desk for emphasis. "It's Mick, Mick Swanson. He's the other owner of *Flash*—our art director and main photographer!"

"Your partner!" Nancy exclaimed.

"Yes." Yvonne patted a stray black hair calmly into place. "But," she hastened to add, "it's not his fault. He can't help himself. You see, I think Mick is cracking up. He's never been very stable, and right now, the pressure of *Flash*'s success is getting to him."

"How do you know he's going over the edge?" Nancy asked.

"Mick and I are old friends," Yvonne explained. "I can tell when he's starting to flip out. In fact, our friendship is the very reason I called you instead of the police. I care about Mick a lot, and I want this thing handled delicately. I don't want any embarrassments— not for Mick and not for *Flash*."

"But why is he threatening you?" Nancy asked.

Yvonne sighed. "To tell the truth, Mick and I have been . . . disagreeing a lot lately. Actually, we've been fighting," she admitted. "It hasn't quite come to out-and-out punching, but almost."

"I see," Nancy said. "Well, then, why now? I mean, why is Mick getting vicious all of a sudden? Has something changed for him recently?"

"Yes!" Yvonne answered, her dark eyes gleaming. "Not just for Mick but for all of us here at *Flash*. Our sales figures are skyrocketing, and that's attracted quite a bit of attention, primarily from MediaCorp, the international news syndicate."

"They want to buy you out?" Nancy asked.

"They've offered us ten million dollars."

"Are you going to accept it?" Nancy leaned forward in her seat, waiting for the answer.

Yvonne's expression remained impassive.

"No way," she said. "*Flash* is my baby. I gave up a writing career for this magazine. I'm not ready to get rid of it yet, not even for a whole lot of money."

Nancy was surprised. This was an emotional side of Yvonne she hadn't figured on. "Then it's Mick who wants to sell," Nancy surmised. "That's why he's been threatening you."

"Not threatening, *trying* to kill me," Yvonne insisted. "But no, Detective Drew," she said with a smile, "I'm afraid you've deduced wrong this time. Mick doesn't want to sell either. But somehow, he's gotten the idea that *I* do! That's the crazy part. Now he's willing to do anything to stop me from selling—even though I don't intend to!"

Nancy felt uncomfortable. She didn't like the way Yvonne seemed to be getting a kick out of her wrong deduction. But good detectives never let emotions distract them when they were looking for clues. Keeping her feelings to herself, Nancy said simply, "That's pretty complicated." She reached across Yvonne's desk to take the letters. "May I—"

"Oh, please, go ahead," Yvonne said, interrupting Nancy.

Nancy picked up the two envelopes. She slipped the first letter out and looked it over carefully. There was no doubt about it—it was frightening.

The letter included a photo. The picture was a still from a horror movie. It showed a brutal-looking man with an ax about to attack some poor woman. But the sender of the letter had replaced the face of the movie actress with Yvonne's own picture. There was a note, too.

Yvonne,

You're mistaken if you think I'm joking. Unless you change your mind about the deal, you're not going to have one to change. There won't be anything you can do to stop me. So just sit back and wait for the pain. It's only a matter of time. . . .

The Grim Reaper

Chapter
Two

$\mathbf{N}$ANCY REREAD THE chilling note. "Pretty gruesome stuff," she said. No wonder Yvonne was so upset.

She turned her attention to the second letter. Immediately, she recognized the words from a top-ten pop song the deejays had been playing practically every two minutes for the past few months.

So you think the evening's pretty
Hey, but you don't know this city
There's always someone hiding in the night
Looking for a victim or a fight
Hiding round the corner out of sight

And that guy will getcha
He'll getcha, he'll getcha
Don't you know he'll getcha . . . soon?

A letter was attached to the lyrics.

Yvonne,
    You've made a bad choice, one you're going to regret. Tell the people you've been doing business with that you won't sell—or else pay the consequences!

                            Your mystery friend,
                            The Grim Reaper

Nancy took another careful look at the two letters. From the perforations on the sides of the paper, she could tell they'd been written on a computer. She made a mental note to check some of the printers in the office and see if the type matched. Still, if all the printers at *Flash* were identical and the letters had been written on one of them, it would be impossible to trace them to one particular machine or another. The notes could also have been written on anybody's home computer. There was a good chance that checking the type would lead nowhere.

"Now do you see why I think Mick's serious about these threats?" Yvonne said earnestly, her dark eyes catching Nancy's blue ones urgently. "I mean, you have to be pretty crazy just to think up stuff that sick. I need help, Nancy, and I hope you're the person to give it to me!" Suddenly Yvonne looked very tired.

Nancy smiled supportively. Obviously, Yvonne was in a terrible situation. Nancy handed the letters back. "I'd like to get these copied," she said.

As she dropped the envelopes onto the desk, she knocked a thin paperback novel to the floor. Leaning down to pick it up, she recognized the title. It was a recent detective novel Nancy herself had enjoyed reading. "Hey," she said, "this is a great book. Are you a mystery fan, too?"

"Oh, *that*," Yvonne said with disdain. "Someone gave it to me the other day, but I can't stand detective stories. They're so predictable."

It was an innocent enough comment, but Nancy picked up a valuable clue from it. She realized that Yvonne liked to make herself seem more mature, more sophisticated, and more intelligent than the people she was around. She was a woman who liked to have the upper hand in her relationships.

Yvonne returned the letters to her desk drawer. "Well, how about it, Nancy?" she asked. "Will you take the case?"

Nancy paused for a moment, thinking. "If I do," she said at last, "I'll need a cov—"

"Of course, you'll need a cover," the publisher broke in. "And I've thought of the perfect one. I'll set you up as an intern. We always need an extra hand around here."

"That might work," Nancy said.

"Sure it will. Do you know anything about photography and camera equipment?"

"Yes," Nancy replied, "I took a summer course last—"

"Great! Then you'll do it?" Yvonne interrupted.

Nancy gave Yvonne a long, appraising look. Throughout their conversation, the publisher had been perfectly polite, but she was always interrupting, as if what she had to say were more important than anything Nancy had to say. And she masked her feelings. Somehow, Nancy didn't trust her.

Still, Nancy told herself, if she really is in danger, she needs me! She flashed the publisher a brilliant smile. "Yes, I'll do it," she said.

"Great!" Yvonne replied.

Nancy leaned back against the black leather couch. "There are still some things I need to know," she told Yvonne. "Background information about you, the magazine, Mick, anyone else who might be involved, too."

"Ask anything you want," Yvonne said.

"Well, can you give me some idea of your past? What have you been doing for the last few years? Who have you been spending your time with?"

Yvonne told Nancy that she'd graduated five years earlier from a small private college. She'd majored in creative writing and, as she'd mentioned before, she'd spent a few years as a novelist before coming up with the idea for *Flash*. She'd given up everything to get the

13

magazine started, and it was finally paying off in record sales figures.

"What about Mick?" Nancy asked. "How did he get involved with *Flash?*"

"I'd met Mick when he was still in art school," Yvonne explained. "I was friends with his roommate at the time. Anyway, he was studying painting—you know, symbolic impressionism and all that. He hadn't gotten into commercial art yet. He was just an idealistic kid. I had to teach him everything," Yvonne went on condescendingly.

"I see," Nancy said drily.

"After Mick got out of college, he went through a hard time. He was emotionally unstable, didn't know what he wanted to do with his life other than paint. Since he was enormously talented, I asked him to join me when I started *Flash.* I thought the work would straighten him out a little," she told Nancy. "I guess I was wrong."

Yvonne gave Nancy a brief history of *Flash* magazine and a rundown on a few of the people who worked there. She said she'd met the current editor in chief, David Bowers, at a party. She'd stolen him away from the prestigious publication he'd been working for at the time. And she'd been dating him since he'd come to work at *Flash* four months ago.

Yvonne said many of the others who worked on the magazine were talented young people on their way up or college students hired as interns. "We like to give new talent a chance," she explained, adding that many of the key positions at the magazine were held by people who had little practical experience but a great commitment to trying out daring creative ideas. Yvonne claimed this was what made *Flash* so successful.

Nancy didn't learn anything more that seemed important, but she'd already found out a lot. She had the feeling that whatever happened, the case was not going to be boring!

"Well," Yvonne said, "how about if I introduce you to your number-one suspect? Mick needs to meet you, too, if I'm going to hire you as an intern."

"I'm ready," Nancy replied, smiling and stretching her legs for a moment.

Yvonne picked up the telephone and pushed a button on the intercom that buzzed Mick's office. "Could you come in here," she said brusquely. There was a pause. "No, it can't wait." She hung up the phone abruptly.

In a few moments, there was a knock on the door, and Mick walked into Yvonne's office. He was tall, blond, good-looking, about twenty-six years old, and very wild! He was wearing a leopard-print jacket, tight black jeans, and black cowboy boots. And I wondered if this sweater dress would be too casual, Nancy thought, hiding a smile.

Mick had finely chiseled features and high cheekbones. In fact, his face would have been perfect if not for his sullen, angry expression.

"All right, Verdi. What's so urgent?" Mick demanded, glaring at Yvonne. "You interrupted me in the middle of something important."

Yvonne glared right back. "Well, this is important, too, Mick," she said.

"I hope so," Mick retorted, "because I don't like being ordered away from my work for nothing."

Yvonne gave a little laugh, as if she could brush off the seriousness of Mick's comments with it. "I asked you in here because I'd like you to meet Nancy Drew, *Flash*'s newest intern— and your new assistant."

Nancy stared at Yvonne in surprise. Yvonne hadn't said anything about being Mick's assistant. Why had she chosen that moment to spring the development on Nancy? Or, for that matter, on Mick? Nancy had never heard of one partner hiring an assistant for another. But the important thing was how Mick was going to react to it. Nancy turned her attention to the art director.

Mick swiveled his cold blue gaze toward Nancy. Suddenly she felt like a lobster in a restaurant fish tank. The art director looked as if he were about to eat her and spit out the shell. There was a moment of deadly silence. Then Mick exploded. *"You hired an assistant for me?* Yvonne, what kind of game are you playing? If I *need* an assistant, I'll hire one myself!"

"Mick," Yvonne cut in smoothly, "you work

awfully hard. I was just trying to do something nice for you."

Nancy sucked in her breath. It looked as if Yvonne and Mick were really into fighting dirty. She could tell that a lot of insults were about to get thrown around.

"Your concern is less than touching," Mick said coldly.

"So is your appreciation, dear. Why don't you just say thank you instead of acting like a spoiled adolescent on an ego trip?"

Nancy glanced at Mick. His handsome face was undergoing an odd transformation, as if he'd lost some kind of inner control. "Yvonne," he said tightly, "you're begging for a fight. And how could I let my dear old partner down? You asked for it. Well, *you're going to get it!*"

Looking Yvonne straight in the eyes, he reached over and picked up a vase on her desk. In one convulsive movement, he crashed the heavy crystal down in front of her, shattering it.

"If you're gonna play games with me," he growled, "get ready to lose—to lose *everything.*"

Chapter

Three

NANCY STARED DOWN at the broken glass which littered Yvonne's carpet, then rested her gaze on the red-faced, trembling Mick. Wow, she thought, he really *is* dangerous! His anger was truly frightening. Without another word, Mick turned on his heel and strode out of Yvonne's office.

For a moment, the publisher stared blankly at the smashed crystal. Nancy almost thought she was going to break down and cry. But then a look of gloating satisfaction stole across Yvonne's face. "You see?" she said. "He doesn't have a hold on himself. Half the time I have the feeling he's about to throw *me* across the room like that."

"That was quite a display of anger," Nancy

agreed cautiously. She picked up a piece of glass and studied it, thinking. It certainly looked as though Yvonne were in danger. But what about Nancy herself? It seemed to her that Mick could easily turn his fury on anybody who was near him. And since Yvonne had so thoughtfully made Nancy his assistant, she was going to be near him quite a bit.

But there was something else. Mick's anger hadn't been unprovoked. Yvonne had goaded him into it. And the nasty comments had come as much from Yvonne as from Mick. The case was complicated, more complicated than Yvonne was making it seem.

"I'd like to make a phone call," Nancy finally said.

"Oh, please, use my telephone," Yvonne offered.

"Uh, no," Nancy replied, trying to think up an excuse quickly. It was never a good idea to talk about a case in front of anyone who was involved—even the person who'd hired you. "You need to clean up here," she said. "I'll use another phone." Nancy got to her feet and scooped her bag off the couch.

"Okay," Yvonne answered. "Mick's going to be starting a photo session pretty soon. We're doing an article on Danielle Artman—you know, the lead singer from that new all-girl rock band, Spiders of Power?"

"Hey, great!" Nancy said enthusiastically, suddenly remembering that *Flash* had a lot more to offer than just the promise of an interesting mystery. "Their single's terrific."

"Well, as Mick's assistant, and as a detective gathering information about a man set on murder, you should be there. So why don't you wait for Mick in the photo studio when you're done with your call?"

"Okay," Nancy agreed.

"And make sure you check in with me often so we can talk about the case." Yvonne began picking up the larger pieces of broken glass.

Nancy hurried out of the office. She rushed past the receptionist and caught the elevator to the ground floor. She found a pay phone and dialed Ned Nickerson's number.

Ned's going to be really upset, she told herself. Still, she couldn't help smiling at the thought of her handsome, longtime boyfriend. Ned was too much in love with her to stay mad for more than a few minutes. No doubt about it, she was lucky to have such an understanding guy.

The phone rang twice before Nancy heard Ned say, "Hello."

"Ned, it's me. And you'll never guess what's up," Nancy said excitedly into the receiver.

"Wait, don't tell me. You're on to another mystery."

"Yes! How did you guess? This time, it looks really serious—maybe even dangerous. I might need your help!" Quickly she recapped the scene in Yvonne's office.

"Nancy," Ned said testily once she had finished, "what about our trip with my parents up to the cabin at the lake? Did you forget all about that?"

"No, of course not," Nancy answered quickly, toying nervously with the cord of the telephone, "but we've got to call that off. We'll go some other time, Ned, I promise."

"Nancy!" Ned sighed with exasperation. "If I had a nickel for every time you've said something like that to me, I could retire right now, a wealthy man."

Nancy was quiet for a moment. It was true, she'd disappointed Ned before. But could she help that she'd rather be working on a mystery than doing just about anything else?

Ned broke the silence. "How important is this, Nancy?"

Nancy sighed. "It's very important. I don't think I could pass it up, Ned. Yvonne's life might be on the line! Besides, this mystery seems really hot."

"I think I'm having déjà vu," Ned moaned. "Last time we were supposed to go up to the cabin, you had to cancel because of some mystery. Now it's happening all over again!"

Nancy tapped her fingers impatiently on the telephone. "But, Ned," she said, "you weren't with me in that office. This guy Mick practically turned green with anger. He's *definitely* violent. If I don't deal with the situation, Yvonne might end up dead!"

But Ned wasn't buying Nancy's argument. "Tell me the truth," he said. "Didn't you tell Yvonne you'd take the case *before* Mick flipped out? When it looked as if it was just a matter of a few nasty letters—nothing too serious?"

Nancy coughed, embarrassed. Ned's been hanging around me too long, she decided. He's becoming a pretty good detective himself. "Okay, you're right," she muttered. "But," she rushed on, "that doesn't change the fact that Yvonne needs me badly."

Ned sighed again. "Right, Nancy. Everybody needs you. I just wish you'd realize that I do, too."

"I know that, silly," Nancy said lightly. "And I hope *you* know how much I love you. And need you, too. Like right now, with this mystery."

"Well," said Ned, hedging, "what have you got in mind?"

"If Mick is going to continue to get violent, I might need some physical protection. A strong, handsome quarterback would be just perfect." Nancy smiled. A little flattery couldn't hurt.

"I don't know. It's not exactly what I had planned for spring break. When I leave Emerson College I really like to get away. I mean, given the choice between hanging around with a bunch of loonies at some magazine office or swimming and sunning with you—"

Nancy frowned. Ned was really holding out. She knew he'd give in in the end (he loved her too much not to), but she hadn't expected to have to work so hard for a simple yes.

"Oh, Ned, say you'll do it." Nancy had run out of arguments. "You're always an incredible help on these cases. I really mean that."

"I don't know why I let you drag me into these things," Ned muttered.

"I love you, Ned. And thanks a lot!" Nancy cried. "You're the best." She threw her boyfriend an over-the-phone kiss and then replaced the receiver. Good old Ned. He never let her down.

Nancy took the elevator back to the sixteenth floor. The same guy was sitting at the reception desk, still playing Clone Wars. "Hi," Nancy said.

"Hi. How's it going? I heard a big crash in Yvonne's office."

"Why didn't you go find out what happened?" Nancy asked curiously. "Someone could have been in trouble."

"Lately," the young man explained, "there's been a lot of yelling coming from Yvonne's and Mick's offices. Mostly when they're alone together. We try not to notice it anymore. As long as they keep their fighting between themselves, none of us really cares."

"I see," Nancy answered.

"So who are you?" the receptionist asked.

Nancy smiled. "I'm Nancy Drew. Yvonne just hired me as an intern. I'm going to be helping Mick out."

"I'm an intern, too," the young man said,

shaking Nancy's hand. "Yvonne likes to hire us because she can give us Mickey Mouse-sized paychecks and make us work like dogs."

Hmmm, Nancy thought. That sure wasn't the way Yvonne had described it. "By the way," the receptionist said, "my name's Scott."

"Nice to meet you. Listen, Yvonne told me to wait for Mick in the studio. Which way is it?"

"All the way at the end of the blue hall. Most of the offices are in that direction. Only Yvonne's and Mick's offices and the darkroom are down the other one."

"Okay. Thanks." Nancy turned down the blue hallway. Ahead of her, she noticed a woman in a tight red dress, walking with a slight swing to her hips. Somehow, she looked familiar to Nancy. The long black hair. And the way she strutted along . . . Oh no, Nancy realized in a flash. It's Brenda Carlton!

Brenda was an amateur reporter who'd gotten in Nancy's way before, practically ruining cases for her on a few occasions. And she was always turning up in the worst places. What's *she* doing here? Nancy wondered. All she needed was blabbermouth Brenda hanging around, blowing her cover and messing with her mystery. What a headache! Impulsively Nancy made a face at Brenda's retreating back.

At least Brenda hadn't seen her—yet. Nancy planned to do her best to keep it that way. She didn't want Brenda ruining things for her before they even got off the ground.

"Hey," Nancy heard someone call from behind her. "Hey, Brenda." Uh-oh, Nancy thought. She's going to turn around. I've got to get out of here!

Nancy looked desperately for a hiding place, but saw only long blue walls and closed office doors. Great. Terrific. Brenda's going to see me—and then I might as well kiss this case goodbye.

Chapter

Four

NANCY DID THE only possible thing. She dashed through the nearest door, went flying into the room beyond, and slammed the door closed behind her. Panting heavily, she raised her eyes to see whom she'd just barged in on. A dark-haired man, about thirty years old, with steely gray eyes, was staring at her angrily.

"All right, who are you and what are you doing in my office?"

"Um, I . . ." Nancy tried desperately to come up with a believable excuse. "I was looking for the studio," she said lamely.

"Well, my dear," the man said sarcastically, "that would be through the double doors at the end of the hall, the ones under the big sign that says Studio."

"Oh," Nancy said.

"What's your name?" the man demanded.

Nancy bit her lip. This was a great way to get a reputation as a dumb redhead around the office. "I'm the new intern, Nancy Drew," she mumbled, trying to smile.

"And *I* am David Bowers," said the man. "I'm the editor in chief of *Flash*. This is my office. And if I catch you coming in here again without knocking first, you're going to be very sorry! Understand?"

Nancy nodded.

"Good." David Bowers turned back to the stack of papers on his desk.

Nancy ducked out of the office quickly. Luckily, Brenda was nowhere in sight.

"Whew," Nancy breathed. So that was Yvonne's boyfriend! What a creep! Of course, she'd acted like a real space cadet, and that wasn't his fault. Still, he could have been a *little* nicer.

It was funny, but David Bowers looked oddly familiar to Nancy. She shook her head. He probably just reminded her of someone she'd met before. However, one thing was becoming painfully obvious to Nancy. With all the bad-tempered people who worked at *Flash*, the case, although exciting, was not going to be pleasant.

Nancy hurried down the hall and pushed open the double doors. The studio was a huge, windowless room. Seamless white paper hung from the ceiling as a backdrop for the photos. Several people were busy setting up cameras, lights, and props for the session. Nancy recognized Scott, the receptionist, struggling with some lighting filters.

A pretty blond girl with delicate features and a great figure was hanging red and black rubber spiders from strings attached to the backdrop. She looked about eighteen.

Turning, the girl saw Nancy and smiled warmly. "Gross, aren't they?" she said with a laugh. "They're in honor of Danielle Artman's band, the Spiders of Power."

"I don't know, they're kind of cute," Nancy joked. "By the way, I'm the new intern, Nancy Drew. I'm supposed to wait here for Mick."

The girl's smile faded. "Oh," she said shortly. "Well, he'll be here soon enough. Why don't you go sit over there"—the girl motioned vaguely—"and wait."

"Can't I help you hang your crawly friends?" Nancy asked.

"I'm doing just fine by myself," the girl replied.

Wow, Nancy thought, do I suddenly have leprosy or something? She moved away from the girl and settled herself cross-legged on the floor. Nancy was beginning to be thankful the job was only temporary.

After a little while, Scott noticed Nancy sitting alone and came over. "Hey, what's happening?"

"Not much. Scott, who's that?" She indicated the yellow-haired girl.

"That's Sondra Swanson, Mick's sister. She's

Flash's stylist. You know, gets celebs ready for shoots, coordinates clothes and prop colors, stuff like that. She does a pretty good job, too. Why?"

"I don't know," Nancy said. "She seemed really friendly when I came in, but as soon as I told her my name, she clammed up."

"That's because she thinks you're a spy," Scott said matter-of-factly.

"A spy!" Nancy cried.

"Yeah. She was just complaining about you. She says she knows exactly how long the waiting list for interns is and that Nancy Drew wasn't next up for a job at *Flash*. In fact, she feels the magazine doesn't even need a new intern right now. So she's decided that Yvonne set you up to spy on her brother. It's really the only logical conclusion."

"Oh, great," Nancy said with a groan. "And what do you think?"

Scott smiled sheepishly. "I think it's a distinct possibility. But," he added quickly, "I don't care. You seem nice, and I'm not getting involved in *Flash* Wars."

Nancy sighed. In a way, it was true. Yvonne really had hired her to spy on Mick. "Thanks for the vote of confidence, Scott. Tell me something else. Do you know who Brenda Carlton is?"

"Sure. She's a free-lance reporter."

"What's she doing at *Flash*?"

"Writing an article on some swimmer who's been tearing it up at high-school meets around the country lately. I think he's a cousin of hers or something."

Nancy scowled. It figured. As usual, Brenda was getting work because of who she knew, not how good a reporter she was. And also as usual, she was sure to get in Nancy's way, probably at the most crucial point in the case.

At that moment, Mick came in. He was talking to a short, curvy girl with shiny brown hair and laughing hazel eyes. Nancy recognized Danielle Artman. She was wearing skintight red pants with a pattern of black spiders on them. "Hey, cool!" she exclaimed. "Your spiders match mine!"

"Sure, that's how I planned it," Sondra said, approaching Danielle with a charming smile.

"Yuck," Mick shuddered. "Sondra, this is by far the most disgusting idea you've ever had for a shoot."

"Don't be scared, brother dear," Sondra teased. "They won't bite." Playfully, she threw a rubber spider at Mick. "He's the world's biggest practical joker," she told Danielle, "but he freaks out over spiders, even fake ones."

Mick batted the bug away. "Disgusting," he repeated with another shudder. He noticed Nancy sitting on the sidelines. "Excuse me, but just because you're Yvonne's latest flunky doesn't mean you can hang around doing nothing," he said. "Help Sondra hang the rest of these spiders so we can start shooting."

Nancy stood up and smiled tentatively, but

Sondra just turned her back. Nancy shrugged and got to work.

Behind her, Mick was checking some camera equipment, singing tunelessly as he worked. "I'll getcha, I'll getcha, you know I'm gonna getcha . . . soon."

That's the song used in the threat letter! Nancy thought. So Mick had two strikes against him. First, he was a photographer and could easily have doctored the picture of Yvonne from a still from the horror movie, and second, he was singing the weird song from Yvonne's letter!

Nancy continued hanging spiders. Soon everything was set for the session, and Mick was ready to begin shooting. "Hey," he shouted at Nancy, "get off the seamless."

"Sure," Nancy said, trying to stay calm and collected as she walked over to where the photo equipment had been set up. She was determined not to show how much Mick's rudeness was getting to her.

"Okay, 'assistant,' I'm going to need you to keep my coffee cup filled and reload the cameras for me when I'm finished with a roll," Mick told Nancy. "You *do* know how to do that, don't you? Or did Yvonne just happen to forget to ask you about those particular skills during your 'interview'?"

"I think I can handle it," Nancy replied coolly. She peered at Mick's camera. "This model is great for shooting moving subjects, better with high-speed film. Gives a grainy picture, so it's not great for portraits." She picked up another camera. "This one is better for portraits and facial shots. Oh, and I see you've got a telephoto lens on it already, so you can get nice close-ups."

Nancy gently replaced the camera on the floor. She knew she was showing off, but it felt good. She was getting very sick of Mick's put-downs.

Mick was glaring at Nancy. "So Yvonne got herself a spy who knows about photography. Great. The least I can get out of you is some decent work."

Mick flicked on the tape deck as Danielle took her place against the white backdrop. An old Rolling Stones song came blasting out of the speakers. "Okay, Danielle," Mick cried. "Let's see some spider action!"

He started clicking his camera as Danielle began moving to the pounding bass beat. She jumped, she wiggled.

"More to the left," Mick called, still shooting. "Beautiful, beautiful. Another jump . . ."

Nancy had to admit Mick knew his stuff. It looked as if he were getting some fantastic shots. Danielle was a great subject to photograph, too. She was very energetic and seemed to have no inhibitions in front of the camera.

With so much action, Nancy barely had time to do any detective work, but she did get a chance to talk to one of the other interns during a five-minute break.

Leslie was a tall black girl about Nancy's age.

She said that she'd been an intern at *Flash* for almost six months. "It's a great job," Leslie said, "if you can get past the cattiness, back-stabbing, and general complaining." She laughed. "Actually, it's not so bad as long as Yvonne stays in her office. She's really awful! Stay clear of her if you can."

"Why is she so terrible?" Nancy asked.

"I think she loves screaming more than anything else in the world. She'll make you do perfectly good work over again for some petty reason. And she's not above nasty personal comments." Leslie made a face. "I mean, I'm willing to put a lot into my job, but my bosses definitely cannot buy me body and soul—not for *this* lousy pay."

Nancy laughed. "How do the other people here feel about her?"

"Oh, about the same, I guess," Leslie answered. "She makes working here real hell. To tell you the truth, I think any one of us would gladly kill that woman if we had the chance."

Nancy caught her breath sharply. You might be more accurate than you know, Leslie, she thought. But she let the comment pass. "I'll try not to let her bother me," she said. "Hey," she added, "I met the editor in chief today."

"Oh, David Bowers. He's another nasty one. He likes pushing people around. He and Yvonne are a perfect pair."

"I thought I'd met him somewhere before," Nancy told the intern. "Do you know anything about him?"

"Yeah—I know he's a big bore. He just came back from two weeks in Rio. And if I hear one more South America story, I'm going to barf." Leslie sighed. "I don't believe that guy. He started working here a few months ago and immediately began trying to impress Yvonne. He had some hot job before he came to *Flash*, but no one knows what it was. He's a mystery man. Where do you think you saw him?"

"I don't know," Nancy said slowly. "I wish I could remember."

"Let me know if you do. I'm dying of curiosity," Leslie said with a smile.

After another hour of nonstop shooting, Mick hit the power button of the tape deck. The studio suddenly went silent. "Okay, Danielle, take a break. Everyone else, get those creepy rubber web-makers off the set as fast as possible. I want to photograph Danielle while she's singing, and I've had just about enough of those things."

Nancy, Sondra, Scott, and a few others got to work cutting down the spiders. Meanwhile, Nancy listened in as Mick talked quietly to the young singer. "Tired?" he asked gently.

"Pooped," Danielle admitted.

"You worked hard and well! You're a natural, Danielle. You've got talent—and not only as a musician. Anyway, we're almost done. Push yourself for just a little longer and then you can rest. You deserve it."

Nancy was surprised to see this considerate

side of Mick. Until then, he'd been nothing but awful. Well, you never know about people, Nancy told herself.

Once the spiders were down and the cameras reloaded, Mick asked Nancy to bring over Danielle's red guitar. Danielle decided to sing a song she'd written called "Give Me Freedom to Speak and a Nice Warm Bed." Nancy thought she really rocked out, too.

When the final strains of Danielle's guitar had faded, Mick ordered the others to take down the seamless. "And you, Nancy," he said, "I want you to stash these spiders in the props closet—way in the back, where I won't have to look at them again."

Nancy dutifully picked up the box of spiders. This time she didn't even notice Mick's rude tone. She was too busy trying to figure out where she'd seen David Bowers before. Suddenly it came to her. Her father, being a famous lawyer, was a regular contributor to *The Midwest Law Review*. About five months earlier, Nancy had gone into the magazine's offices with her father. She'd met David there briefly. He'd been editor in chief at the time. No big deal. Except that, if Nancy remembered correctly, *The Midwest Law Review* was owned by none other than MediaCorp!

That seemed like a very important link to Nancy, since the company was presently trying to buy out *Flash* and was causing big problems between Yvonne and Mick because of it. Was

David's last job common knowledge? Was he still connected with MediaCorp? This could be a key to the case!

Suddenly Nancy was no longer so sure that Mick was behind the letters. The evidence against him was purely circumstantial. Since the threatening song was on the radio a couple of times every day, it wasn't so strange that Mick should sing it. And Mick wasn't the only photographer on the *Flash* staff. Lots of people could have doctored the movie still. Nancy herself was capable of it. Furthermore, from the way Leslie had talked, just about everyone in the office had a motive!

Nancy headed for the props closet. "Make sure you put those things *all* the way in the back," Mick called after her.

Nancy opened the closet door and pushed past wacky costumes, designer clothes, and a strange collection of miscellaneous objects that had been used as props for other shoots. But what was that on the floor? Drops of blood?

Nancy moved aside a few evening dresses—and saw something that made her crawl! Sitting on top of an old chest of drawers was a severed head! A finely honed ax was suspended in the air next to it.

As Nancy looked up, the ax began to fall—right toward her face.

Chapter

Five

Nancy stared in horror as the ax fell toward her head. At the very last moment, she jumped out of the way like a race-car driver bailing out before a crash.

The ax hurtled to the floor—and bounced! It was made out of rubber!

Nancy gasped. A queasy mixture of anger, fear, and relief washed over her. She bent down and examined the toy ax. The blade was rubber, but the handle was hard wood. Some practical joke, Nancy thought. If that thing had hit her, the handle could have knocked her out, rubber blade or no rubber blade. She reached up to touch the "severed head" and found that it was an incredibly convincing mask. She picked up the ax and quietly walked out to the studio.

When she appeared, Mick started laughing

wildly. "Mick, the remote control whiz kid, strikes again," he joked, oblivious to Nancy's distress. "Simple but brilliant," he bragged. "I rigged a remote control device to the handle of that ax. Then all I had to do was push a button to make it fall." He laughed again and pulled a small control box out of a jacket pocket.

"Hey, Mick," Sondra called to her brother, "what'd you do? Pull another one of your sick practical jokes? Why don't you cut that junk out already? People get upset by it."

Mick snickered. "Oh, Nancy didn't mind too much, did you, Nancy?" Not waiting for an answer, he continued, "This one was really great, if I may say so myself." He turned to Nancy and gave her a twisted smile.

Self-possessed as always, Nancy didn't show how much Mick's joke had bothered her. But she wondered whether it was a gruesome warning to stay off his tail, or just his way of asserting his power. After all, Nancy told herself, he *is* co-owner. Maybe he likes letting the staff know he can do anything he wants around here, anything at all. If so, Mick was treating *Flash* like his personal playroom.

One thing was for sure. Mick's violent side was becoming more and more obvious.

Mick threw Nancy another sharkish grin. Then he turned to the rest of the staff. "Good shoot," he told them. "You all worked hard." He motioned to Danielle to come with him, and together they left the studio.

As soon as her brother was gone, Sondra hurried over to Nancy. "I'm really sorry about that," she said. She seemed sincere, but still a little wary of Nancy. "What did he pull this time?"

Nancy described what she'd seen in the closet. "I don't scare easily," she said, "but I have to admit, I was pretty flipped out just now."

"Wow, that sounds awful!" Sondra murmured apologetically, her blue eyes opening wide. "I wish that hadn't happened."

"Me, too!" Nancy exclaimed.

"Mick's into sick jokes," Sondra explained. "I know it's a drag, but don't take it personally. He does stuff like that to all the new interns." She sighed. "The trouble is, lately, he's been taking his jokes too far." She looked at Nancy with embarrassment. "I . . . I'm sorry."

Nancy smiled graciously. "I'm okay, Sondra. And, by the way, I appreciate the apology."

By that time, the backdrop had been removed and all the equipment put away. Nancy and Sondra left the studio together. "Mick asked me to take you to the darkroom so we can develop the film from today's shoot," Sondra told Nancy.

"Okay," Nancy replied. "That sounds like fun. I'm sure I'm going to learn a lot working here."

"Yeah, that's one of the best things about this company," Sondra agreed. "Anyway, I'll show you where we keep everything and help you with the first few rolls. And if you do a good job, I'll let you finish up alone. I've got a lot of other work to do."

Nancy found that the darkroom was beautifully designed and extensively equipped. After developing one roll of film, Sondra could tell that Nancy knew what she was doing and left her to finish the rest by herself.

Nancy developed film all afternoon, following the written instructions Mick had given Yvonne. He wanted certain rolls developed differently than others, colors brightened or changed. At the end of his letter, he'd added a note to Nancy.

Make sure your careful not to breathe in the chemicals. Their dangerous if you spend too much time in the darkroom. Takes breaks if your feeling funny.

Nancy was once again surprised at the more considerate side of Mick. What did it all mean? Had the incident in the studio really been just a joke? Was the violence in Yvonne's office only a reaction to Yvonne's own rudeness? Or was Nancy dealing with a psycho? Everyone had heard about cases of split personality, people who could switch from being kind and calm to maniacs in just a moment. Suddenly, she wasn't sure *what* to think of Mick.

Nancy read Mick's note over and started to laugh. "Wow," she couldn't help saying out loud. "This guy has the worst spelling in the whole world!" He didn't know the difference between *your* and *you're* or *their* and *they're*.

Nancy rolled up the sleeves of her sweater dress and continued to work on the pictures. She had to admit that Mick was a great photographer. He'd really captured Danielle's spirit—her energy and personality—on film.

It was almost five o'clock by the time Nancy finished her work. As she passed the door to the publisher's office, Yvonne appeared. "Come in for a minute," she said with a smile. "I want to know how your first day went."

"Pretty well," Nancy replied. She closed the door behind her. "I think my cover works. But one of your reporters, Brenda Carlton, knows who I am."

Yvonne shrugged. "No problem. She's hardly ever around the office."

"One more thing," said Nancy. "Do you think there might be an extra intern's job for a guy named Ned Nickerson? He's my assistant."

Surprisingly, Yvonne wasn't keen on the idea. Nancy had figured she'd be thrilled to have an extra pair of detective's eyes searching for the killer, but she wasn't. Still, after a little hard selling from Nancy, she agreed.

Nancy also copied the threat letters and checked a few of the computer printers in the offices to see if the type matched that of the letters. Sure enough, it was identical. And that meant that, if they had been written at the *Flash* offices, it would be impossible to trace the letters to any one person.

Nancy cleaned up the darkroom. After she'd put everything away, she said goodbye to several people and got ready for the train ride back to River Heights.

But when Nancy stepped out of the building into the fading afternoon sunlight, she noticed a familiar figure waiting for her. Tall, toned, and terrific-looking, it was Ned Nickerson. "Hey, honey!" he called.

"Ned!" Nancy cried, melting happily into her boyfriend's arms.

"Mmm," Ned said, giving Nancy a long, lingering kiss.

"Mmm," Nancy replied, kissing Ned back and staring blissfully into his soft, dark eyes as she ran her fingers through his fine, light brown hair.

At last the couple broke apart. "What are you doing here?" Nancy asked.

"What do you mean?" Ned teased. "We haven't seen each other since yesterday. The loneliness was killing me! And what else do I have to do on a beautiful Wednesday afternoon besides drive into Chicago and pick up my gorgeous girlfriend?"

Then Ned's handsome face became serious. "Actually, Nancy, I was a little worried about you. After our phone conversation this afternoon, I started having horrible thoughts about that guy you told me about." Ned flashed Nancy a tender smile. "And I'm sorry we argued."

"It was nothing compared to what I went

through at the office!" Nancy exclaimed. As they climbed into Ned's car and headed for the suburbs, she told him what had happened, from Brenda Carlton and David Bowers to Mick and his sick sense of humor and Sondra's apology.

"Sondra sounds nice," Ned commented when Nancy had finished.

"I guess she is," Nancy admitted, "but I have a feeling she doesn't want to make things any easier for me. She seems to think I'm Yvonne's latest pet." Nancy rolled down the car window and let the spring air blow through her hair.

"You can't really blame her for that," Ned said.

"No," Nancy agreed. "Anyway, this case is a little frightening—but very intriguing."

"I don't know, Nancy." Ned was doubtful. "I'd say the accent is on dangerous. I mean, Mick may already be on to your true identity. Maybe we should just go to the police and let them handle it."

"No," Nancy argued. "Right now, a crime hasn't even been committed. There've been a few nasty letters, a few ugly fights, a practical joke. None of that's very out of the ordinary for a high-pressure office like *Flash.*"

"Right," Ned said sarcastically. "People leave severed heads in office closets all over Chicago."

"Come on, Ned, you can't expect me to give up the case before I've found even one concrete clue, can you?"

"But, Nancy," Ned protested, "this Mick

character might be a real nut case. You could be putting your life on the line."

"If I thought that," Nancy answered, "I'd have you pull over at the next roadside diner and I'd call the police immediately. You know, you're making the most simple mistake a detective possibly can—you're assuming the obvious. Mick *might* be the person behind the threats, but it could be just about anyone at *Flash*."

"Great! So there are a *bunch* of violent lunatics over there, not just one," Ned muttered.

"By the way," Nancy said, "I asked Yvonne about hiring you as another intern. It was funny, but she was pretty hesitant at first. Anyway, I convinced her that I really needed you, and she said okay."

Ned sighed, keeping his eyes on the road. "I still think we'd be better off at my parents' cabin."

Nancy caught her breath. "So that's what all this is about. You're just upset about missing our trip!"

"Hey," Ned said, getting annoyed, "I happen to want to spend a little time with the girl I love. What's wrong with that?"

"I don't know," Nancy replied, her temper beginning to flare. "It seems as if you're being selfish. I mean, who cares about some stupid vacation when a person's life might be in danger?"

Ned took his eyes off the road just long enough to give Nancy a look of disbelief. "And who cares about some stupid boyfriend," he said, returning his eyes miserably to the highway, "when you could be running around, getting yourself killed by an art director with an ax to grind? You know, Nancy, I don't think you appreciate me very much."

"Look, I need to do this, Ned. Okay?" Nancy said shortly.

Ned frowned. "No other guy in the world would put up with this, Nancy. And sometimes, I wonder why *I* do."

Chapter
Six

NANCY STARED AT the floor numbers over the elevator door as they lit up, one after another. It was a gray Thursday morning, and she was about to begin her second day of work at *Flash*. The weather suited her state of mind—dark and cool.

Her fight with Ned had upset her, and she hadn't slept well. She was in no mood for the fighting and nastiness that had gone on at the magazine the day before.

Luckily, Ned would be there now to help handle any really sticky situations. In spite of their argument, he was going to work at the magazine, just as he'd promised.

Or maybe that wasn't luck. Ned hadn't been the greatest conversationalist on the train ride into the city that morning. Obviously, he was still mad about the canceled trip. But Nancy knew she had to push her problems with Ned out of her mind. She couldn't let them interfere with the case.

Nancy had left Ned a few blocks away from the building where *Flash*'s offices were housed. She'd decided that they'd get a lot more information if they pretended they didn't know each other. That way, they could search for clues separately. And with luck, Mick and Sondra wouldn't think Ned was a spy. Because of their feelings for Nancy, they definitely weren't going to open up with her. Maybe Ned could get closer to them.

The elevator reached the sixteenth floor, and the doors slid open. Nancy stepped out. Okay, *Flash*, she thought. I'm ready for whatever you've got in store for me today. She walked over to the reception desk. "Hi, Scott," she said.

"Hey, Nancy, how's it going today?"

"Okay, I suppose," Nancy replied noncommittally.

"Well, I hate to be the bearer of bad news, especially so early in the morning, but Mick wants to see you in his office right away."

"Oh." Nancy frowned. She was sure it wasn't going to be very much fun. On the other hand, it was her first real chance to talk to her prime suspect. If she were lucky, she'd pick up a clue or two.

Scott flashed Nancy a sympathetic smile. "I'm really sorry about what Mick put you through yesterday. It's too bad, because actually Mick can be a pretty nice guy at times. Anyway, he said to send you in to him as soon as you got here."

"Thanks." Nancy hung her coat in the closet behind Scott's desk. She'd been a little nervous about what to wear that day. *Flash* was a fashion magazine, after all. Finally she'd chosen a favorite rose-colored sweater that brought out the red highlights in her hair and some classic, tailored black pants with low-heeled pumps.

Nancy headed for Mick's office. She soon found out that it was just as wild as Mick himself. It was decorated with dozens of remote control toys and tacky plastic things, a complete contrast to Yvonne's high-class image. Mick had everything from toy airplanes that really flew to barking dogs and marching soldiers.

Mick was reclining in a big orange armchair when Nancy came in. His feet were on his desk, displaying a pair of zebra-striped shoes. He was wearing an oversized white suit and a zebra ascot around his neck.

"Hi," Mick said. "Have a seat."

"Thanks," Nancy answered. She walked across the room, almost slipping on the highly polished wooden floors.

"Careful," Mick said.

Nancy smiled cautiously, settling into an orange chair identical to Mick's. Obviously Mick was trying to be pleasant and considerate. But why?

"Nancy," he began. He coughed, embarrassed, and swung his feet off the desk. "I've got something to say to you. It's not easy for me but—well, I've got to apologize to you for yesterday. I'm really sorry."

Nancy stared at Mick in surprise. Was this the same guy who'd humiliated her in the studio? The same guy who'd angrily smashed Yvonne's vase to bits?

"My sister was on my case about that joke all night," he continued. "She told me it was completely sick and creepy and that you could have been really scared. Well, I didn't mean it that way. Who'd leave a real severed head in a props closet? I figured you'd realize it was a joke as soon as you saw the head."

Nancy wasn't sure what to make of Mick's apology. He certainly seemed to mean it. But where had the nice Mick been hiding the day before? Was he trying to gain Nancy's trust so he could throw her off his trail?

Actually, Nancy thought, Mick had been considerate with Danielle Artman yesterday. And he'd showed concern about her working all afternoon in the darkroom. Still, that didn't mean the vicious Mick didn't exist, too.

Nancy smiled slowly. "Thanks for the apology," she said simply. "I appreciate it. I *was* pretty worried about all the fighting that went on yesterday."

Mick pressed his lips together. "That's another thing I want to apologize for—my outburst in Yvonne's office. I shouldn't have stuck you in the middle of my fight with Yvonne. And I shouldn't have taken my frustrations with her out on you yesterday in the studio."

"I won't argue with that," Nancy joked. She smiled at Mick sincerely for the first time, realizing that her feelings about the art director were changing. Sure, he was more than a little thoughtless, but he no longer seemed like the crazy, malicious person Nancy had first taken him for. He'd behaved badly, and he was apologizing for it. Nancy thought that was honorable. Mick would probably be a really nice guy, Nancy decided, if he hadn't gotten successful so young.

"Well," said Mick, "you've just got to understand that I never asked for an assistant." The bitterness was clear in his tone. "Yvonne is driving me insane. She hired you just because it suits some weird plan of her own."

"It *was* kind of bizarre that she made me your assistant without telling you about it first," Nancy admitted.

"Anyway," Mick continued, "as long as you and I are going to be working together, we've got to try to get along. I mean, my problems with Yvonne and MediaCorp aren't your fault."

"MediaCorp," Nancy said, playing innocent. "Isn't that the international news syndicate? They own just about every newspaper and magazine on the East Coast."

"Right, and if I don't watch out, they're going to own *mine,* too," Mick told her. "But I'm not going to let that happen."

Nancy decided to ask Mick a few more questions about MediaCorp. A master at getting information from people without their even knowing it, she set to work. She stretched her long legs and leaned back in her chair, hoping to make Mick feel less formal.

"I used to know someone," the sleuth said easily, "who worked for MediaCorp. Editor in chief at the *Law Review,* I think."

"I hope he wasn't a good friend," Mick said with the hint of a smile. "I wouldn't trust anyone connected with that place."

"Then you wouldn't hire anyone who'd once worked for MediaCorp?" Nancy asked.

"No way," Mick told her. "I hope your friend doesn't want a job here."

"Oh, no," Nancy said quickly. Her mind was racing.

So Mick doesn't know about David's old job, she realized. But Yvonne probably did! There was no way she'd hire an editor in chief without knowing his background. Yvonne was that kind of person. And she must have hidden David's background from Mick.

Nancy pursed her lips pensively. She wondered if anyone else around *Flash* knew about David—and if not, why not? She let her eyes wander around the office as if they could somehow discover a clue.

Suddenly she noticed something that made her break into a huge grin. Mick had a whole library of mystery novels displayed on shelves near his desk. "You must be a fellow mystery lover," she said with a laugh, pointing to the books.

"Definitely," Mick said enthusiastically. "I've been reading thrillers ever since I discovered the Hardy Boys back in grade school."

"Yeah, I always loved them, too," Nancy smiled. "I've been reading a lot of Raymond Chandler lately."

"I guess Agatha Christie is still the great master for me," Mick confided. "There's always some bizarre twist in her stories that no one else would ever come up with."

Nancy had to smile. Who would have guessed that Mick was a mystery freak just the way she was? If I don't watch it, she warned herself, I may end up actually getting friendly with Mick.

Mick stood up and extended his hand to Nancy. "You know, you're okay," he said.

Nancy smiled and shook Mick's outstretched hand. Mick had become human to her that morning—which would help her predict his next move if he really were the culprit.

"You did a good job developing that film yesterday, Nancy. This afternoon I'd like you to help Leslie do a preliminary layout for the next issue. Think you can handle it?"

"I'll do my best," Nancy said. "See you later."

Nancy left Mick's office and walked toward the reception desk. She felt that she'd made some important discoveries about the case.

Now if she could just figure out what it all meant!

Nancy entered the reception area. Scott was nowhere in sight, but Ned was there, talking to Sondra and acting very interested in what she was saying. They were standing close. In fact, it looked to Nancy as though her tried-and-true boyfriend were flirting! At that moment, Sondra let out a peal of laughter and Ned broke into a charming smile.

How could Sondra make a play for Ned? Nancy wondered indignantly. Then she remembered Sondra had absolutely no way of knowing she was going after Nancy's boyfriend. But *Ned* should know better!

Still, Nancy had to give Ned the benefit of the doubt. Maybe he was just trying to get information and pick up clues from Sondra. But there was no reason for him to stand so close to her in order to do it. No way was she going to stand around and watch her boyfriend flirt with another girl!

Nancy took two steps forward. And at that moment, two piercing screams cut through the morning calm.

Chapter

Seven

"THAT WAS YVONNE!" Nancy cried. She made a dash for the publisher's office, Ned and Sondra momentarily forgotten. What could have happened?

Nancy threw open the door. Yvonne was standing by her desk, staring horrified into one of its drawers.

"Yvonne!" Nancy exclaimed. "Are you all right?"

"I—I thought it was just a toy until it moved," Yvonne gasped.

Nancy glanced around. Most of the *Flash* staff had followed her into Yvonne's office. Ned and Sondra were right behind her. Mick looked on uncertainly and David's steel-gray eyes surveyed the commotion impassively.

Nancy crossed the room and peered into

Yvonne's desk. At first she didn't see what had scared the publisher. Then something started to crawl. It was a huge, hairy black spider with pinkish legs—a tarantula!

"Where did this come from?" Nancy asked softly, leaning closer to examine the spider.

"I d-don't know," Yvonne sputtered. "I just opened the drawer and there it was!"

Nancy picked up an empty coffee mug and laid it in the desk drawer, its rim facing the spider. She prodded the creature with the end of a pencil until it began crawling into the cup. "We'd better save this for evidence."

But Yvonne pushed by, a paperweight in her hand. "No way am I going to leave that thing hanging around here!" She brought the weight down on the spider.

Nancy stared for a second. But by that time Sondra had already begun yelling at her brother. Of course, Nancy thought with a little mental shrug. This is *Flash*. Why did I expect to get through the morning without at least one major fight?

"Mick, how *could* you?" Sondra was crying. "Yvonne might have been bitten! You are taking these practical jokes way too far. They're not funny anymore!"

A look of confusion, fear, and hurt crossed Mick's face. "Wait a minute, Sondra. Are you saying *I'm* responsible for this? You think I'm crazy or something?"

"Well, who else could it be? No one else around here pulls creepy jokes."

"I'd never get *near* that miserable spider." Mick shuddered. "The rubber ones you brought in for Danielle Artman were bad enough. Besides, I'm not into dangerous jokes. You know that!"

Nancy watched the exchange closely. Mick really did seem shocked that his sister would assume he was responsible. Then again, maybe he was just a very good actor.

Suddenly Nancy remembered that David had just come back from South America. Isn't it interesting, Nancy thought. That's one of the areas where you can find tarantulas. With his connection to MediaCorp, the editor in chief was beginning to look more than a little suspicious.

In ones and twos, the others left the office. Nancy was by no means too wrapped up in the case to miss Ned and Sondra walking out together, but right then there wasn't a thing she could do about it. Last to leave were Mick, still clearly upset by his sister's accusation, and David, who gave Yvonne a kiss on the cheek first.

"How are you feeling?" Nancy asked Yvonne as soon as everyone had cleared out of the office.

"A little shaken," the publisher replied, dropping heavily into her chair. "But okay, I guess."

"This is something I think the police should know about immediately," Nancy said, taking a seat on the leather couch. "I don't have a single concrete clue, so I have no way of judging the situation, but I do know one thing—this case has gone far beyond practical jokes."

Yvonne caught her breath sharply. "No," she said with a fierceness that surprised Nancy. "The reason I hired you was to keep the police out of this. I told you, I'm worried about Mick. I want to keep him out of any serious trouble."

"It looks as if you're getting yourself into some, though," said Nancy.

"But, Nancy, maybe Mick just wanted to scare me."

Nancy sighed. Yvonne was so sure Mick was behind the things that had happened at *Flash*. But until that was proven, Nancy was going to keep her eyes open for any and all possible suspects.

"Whoever planted that spider may or may not have known that it wouldn't kill you," Nancy replied. "Most people think tarantulas are deadly, like black widow spiders, but they're not. In fact, a lot of people keep tarantulas as exotic pets without any problems. This one probably came from a pet store. But the thing is, we still don't know if the person we're looking for is just trying to scare you or if we're up against a murder attempt. That's exactly why I think we should call in the police. We don't have enough information."

"My point exactly. The police aren't

interested in suspicions and possibilities. They want facts, crime victims, switchblade knives. They'll come in here, look around, and do nothing at all. Meanwhile, Mick and *Flash* will have to bear the media coverage that would follow."

Nancy sighed. Yvonne was right. Still, she was a detective, not a bodyguard. She didn't want to feel responsible if another murder attempt occurred and Yvonne got hurt.

Suddenly Yvonne's face softened. "Please," she said, almost pleading, "I want you to handle this yourself. For me, for Mick, and for *Flash*. The next time Mick does something dangerous, we'll call the police, okay?"

"If you're still alive," Nancy replied wryly.

Yvonne broke into a smile. "Great. I knew you'd understand, Nancy. Now I'm going home for a while. I need to cool out after all this."

"Okay," Nancy said, getting to her feet. "Do you mind if I have a look around your office? Maybe the culprit left a clue."

"Go right ahead." Yvonne stood up and got her coat from the closet. "I'll lock the door. Then just close it behind you when you leave." Yvonne slipped into her coat, gathered together a few papers, pushed them into her briefcase and, saying goodbye to Nancy, hurried out.

Nancy got right to work, checking Yvonne's desk drawers first. When she found nothing, she searched the closet and Yvonne's private bathroom. She even looked beneath the cushions of the couch. It was only when she got down on her hands and knees on the floor, peering into every corner, that she found something. One of the large white buttons from Mick's suit was lying underneath the desk.

Nancy picked it up. Then, brushing off her pants, she stood up.

It was a small clue. It didn't prove anything. Mick was in and out of Yvonne's office a few times a day. He may not have lost the button while planting the spider, but it was a possibility.

Nancy decided she needed more definite clues, clues she just might find in Mick's office. She knocked on his door. "It's Nancy," she called.

"Come on in," Mick called back.

Nancy opened the door. "Hi," she said.

"Strange happenings at *Flash,* huh?" Mick said. "I bet you never had a job like this before, did you?" He was joking, but there was a nervous edge to his voice.

"No," Nancy said honestly, "I never have." Now that she was in his office, she had no idea how to get Mick out in order to search it. Well, she told herself, I'll just have to wing it.

"So what can I do for you?" Mick asked.

"Um," Nancy stalled, "I wanted to—to

59

ask you if there was anything I can do for you since Yvonne has gone home."

"No," Mick said, "just go help Leslie with those layouts."

"Okay," Nancy answered. She turned to leave. All at once she slipped on the shiny wood floor and fell flat on her rear. "Ow!" she cried.

"Nancy!" exclaimed Mick. "Here, let me help you. Are you hurt?"

"I think I twisted my ankle," Nancy replied. She allowed Mick to help her limp to the orange armchair. "I don't think it's too bad, but do you think you could get me some ice to put on it? A dancer friend of mine swears it's the best thing for this kind of injury."

"Sure," Mick said, concerned. "There's some in the refrigerator. It's just down the hall. I'll be right back." He dashed out of the room, slamming the door behind him.

As soon as he had gone, Nancy jumped out of the chair. Mick would be gone for just a few minutes. She'd probably only have time to search his desk.

Nancy looked carefully through a few drawers. Nothing. But then she noticed something on top of the desk that was very interesting indeed.

It was a paperback mystery called *Deadly Potion, Deadly Bite* by an author named Ivan Green. Nancy had read it herself, and the story stuck in her mind because of the bizarre way the murderer had killed his victims. He'd used poisons—all different types, including poison from insects!

Wow, Nancy thought. Yvonne finds a tarantula in her desk while Mick's reading a fictional account of the same kind of crime. Was it just a coincidence?

She heard a noise in the hall and glanced at the door. There was Mick's jacket, hanging from a hook. Nancy grabbed the lapel to check the front of the jacket. A button *was* missing!

Dashing back to the armchair, she dropped into it just as Mick returned.

"I brought you a whole bag full of ice," Mick announced.

"Thanks," Nancy said. She spent a few minutes holding the ice to her perfectly normal ankle, her mind speeding from clue to clue all the while. Once again, things were looking bad for Mick. But what about David? Nancy knew she would have to search his office, too, before she completely condemned Mick. She'd need Ned's help for that.

Nancy lost precious time getting Mick to believe she was all right, but at last she made her getaway. She found Ned alone in the photocopy room, duplicating some articles. "Glad to see you've separated yourself from Sondra Swanson long enough to get a little work done," she said sarcastically.

"Nancy—" Ned cried.

But Nancy wouldn't let Ned get another word

out of his mouth. "I need your help. Do you think you can keep David Bowers busy for fifteen minutes or so? I've got to search his office."

"Piece of cake," Ned said, pulling his copies out of the machine. "But listen. Sondra—"

"Forget it," Nancy said. "We don't have time to talk now. See you in a bit." And with that, she hurried out of the room.

Nancy gave Ned five minutes to get David out of his office. Then she snuck in herself. If David catches me here, she thought, I'm dead. She went straight to his desk. The top drawer held pencils, pens, typing paper, and other standard office supplies.

In the second drawer Nancy found a few old greeting cards and a couple of low-quality novels. Obviously, the big-shot editor didn't want anyone to know he liked to read junk, since he hadn't put the books on his shelf next to the leatherbound classics. Nancy couldn't help but giggle to herself about that.

But it was in the bottom drawer that Nancy found something really interesting. It was a note from a top officer at MediaCorp! "Here's the check for that last free-lance job," it said. "Let me know how the new job is going."

Nancy pawed through the papers in the drawer, but she couldn't find the check. David had probably already cashed it. Anyway, she didn't really need it. She had the most important information. She knew that David was still working for MediaCorp! But as a free-lance editor—or as a hired assassin? Nancy's mind reeled with new possibilities.

Nancy knew MediaCorp wanted *Flash*. But how badly? Could they really be as unscrupulous as Nancy was beginning to suspect? How far would a major corporation go to acquire a magazine they wanted? . . . As far as murder?

Chapter

Eight

THE QUESTION OF MediaCorp's possible in-
volvement in the trouble at *Flash* stayed with
Nancy all Thursday afternoon and into the next
morning. The thought scared her. In her many
cases, she'd never come up against such a
powerful criminal. MediaCorp wasn't a human
being—it was an institution. And how did you
fight an institution?

Worse than that, Nancy still wasn't sure the
news syndicate *was* behind the threats. Then
there was Mick. Slowly she was beginning to
think he might be a pretty nice guy. But there
was also plenty of evidence against him. He had
such a complicated personality that Nancy had
no idea how far she could trust him.

Nancy did know one thing for certain. The
plan to have Ned help her on the case had really

backfired. All he seemed to do was hang around with Sondra. He hadn't brought in a single clue yet.

So, after a long Friday morning of hard work, worrying, and not much detective work, Nancy knew she'd be glad to get out of *Flash* at lunchtime—and even gladder that her two best friends, George Fayne and Bess Marvin, were coming into the city from River Heights for a lunch date with her. Nothing soothed troubles like complaining to your best friends.

Just before noon, Scott buzzed Nancy on the office intercom and told her that George and Bess had arrived. Nancy carefully put away her work and headed for the reception area. She bumped into Ned as she was stepping out of the interns' office.

"Nancy," he said, catching her arm, "we've got to talk. You've been avoiding me, and I want to know why."

Ned's eyes caught Nancy's for a moment, but she quickly looked away. It was true, she *was* avoiding him. She'd purposely stayed late at *Flash* the night before just so she wouldn't have to take the train back to River Heights with him. She'd felt horrible about it, but she just hadn't been able to face a heavy discussion about Sondra or their relationship when she had the case on her mind.

"I know we have to talk," Nancy told Ned, "but not right now. George and Bess are waiting for me." She tried to shake off his hand.

"Okay," Ned said calmly, not letting go. "Then when? This is important, you know."

"I'm not sure," Nancy replied, beginning to feel annoyed. "I've got a lot of work to do. I don't have the time to sit around talking—and flirting with cute blonds." She looked up suddenly, her gaze angry and challenging.

But Ned was getting angry, too. "Why don't you stop being so jealous and *think* a little, Nancy? You're supposed to be a detective. Did it ever cross your mind that I might be hanging out with Sondra because the girl I really want to spend time with is too busy?"

"And did it ever cross your mind that I asked you to be an intern to do more than just socialize? Where's all the help you promised me?"

"Oh, come on, Nancy. You've got a free hour or two to have lunch with George and Bess. But when was the last time we had any fun together? I mean, who am I supposed to have lunch with today?"

Nancy felt defensive and guilty and angry all at once. She knew she'd been taking Ned for granted lately. She'd canceled out on the lake trip and she hadn't tried to make up for it in any way. Still, *he* was the one who was spending time with somebody else, so who was he to complain?

"Look, Bess and George are waiting for me," Nancy said, shrugging off the issue. "We'll have to talk some other time."

Ned pressed his lips into a thin, angry line.

"Okay, Nancy. If that's the way you want it." Resignedly, he dropped his hand from Nancy's arm and turned to walk away.

Suddenly Nancy felt as if she were losing Ned. And no matter what was going on between them, he was very precious to her. "Ned," she called, "we'll talk this afternoon, all right?"

But Ned didn't answer. He just stalked off. Nancy heaved a huge sigh and went to meet George and Bess at the reception desk. She knew that if she had to be alone for more than five minutes, she'd probably start to cry.

Nancy found her friends talking to Scott. It looked suspiciously as though Bess were flirting with him. "Bess, George," Nancy said, putting up a happy front. "You two look great!"

Bess's straw-blond hair was fixed in tiny braids, which she'd gathered together in a ponytail. She was wearing a pink skirt and pink high heels—Bess was self-conscious about being shorter than her two friends.

George was her usual down-to-earth self, wearing gray corduroy pants and a matching V-necked sweater that showed off her beautifully toned athlete's body. Her short dark hair fell in soft curls.

"You're not doing too badly yourself," George said. "Especially with this neat job. Really, Nancy, I'm jealous," she said with a smile.

"So where do you want to eat?" Bess asked. "I'm starved!"

"I thought you were on a diet," George teased.

"I am. That's why I'm so hungry."

Nancy laughed, her dark mood easing. "You guys are impossible!"

Nancy suggested a little restaurant not far from *Flash*. It was decorated with big colorful posters and had sunny windows that looked out onto the street.

"So," George said after they had been seated at a corner table and had ordered their lunches. "*Flash* seems like a wild place. The receptionist was playing games on his fancy computer, and some guy walked by wearing the weirdest hat I've ever seen."

"That was probably Mick Swanson," said Nancy. "He's one of my prime suspects."

"Totally gorgeous, too," Bess giggled. "Maybe I could help rehabilitate him from a life of crime."

"He's too old for you, Bess," Nancy said with a laugh.

At that moment the waiter brought over the food. Nancy and George had ordered lasagna, Bess had ordered a low-cal green salad.

Bess sighed and picked at her lettuce. "You guys are so lucky," she said. "You can order whatever you want and never gain an ounce, while I eat nothing but salad and look like a horse."

George cut into her lasagna. "Bess, you are not fat. Lazy, yes. But positively, definitely not fat. I don't know why you're so obsessed with your weight."

"Easy for you to say, Super Athlete. You probably work off calories just thinking about your early morning jogs." Bess stabbed a slice of cucumber and stuffed it into her mouth.

George laughed. Then she turned to Nancy and demanded, "All right, what's going on?"

"What do you mean?" Nancy asked, a little taken aback by the suddenness of her friend's question.

"You've barely said a word today—and when you have, it's been with all the joy of a beauty queen with chicken pox. Now what gives?"

Nancy sighed, pushing her lasagna around her plate. "I guess this case has me a bit down. Someone's doing nasty things to Yvonne so she won't sell the magazine—which she doesn't intend to do anyway. And I'm up against a murderous corporation, a maniacal photographer, or a malicious practical joker, but I have no idea which one."

"Don't give me that," George said. "No matter how confusing a case is, it never gets you as down as you are now."

Nancy smiled. "You know me too well. Okay, it's Ned."

"What's going on with Old Reliable now?" Bess asked sharply.

A little giggle escaped from Nancy's throat. "Yeah, that's how I always thought of him, too. He'd be around for me no matter what I did.

But believe it or not, Ned Nickerson is stepping out on me! Crazy, isn't it?"

"Who is the witch, anyway?" Bess wanted to know.

"Her name's Sondra Swanson. Blond, gorgeous, and, to be honest, kind of nice. She doesn't know Ned and I are involved with each other, so I can't even blame her for going after him. All I can say is that she has good taste in guys."

"Wait a sec," George said, swallowing a bite of food. "Swanson. Isn't that the name of the man with the funny hat? The person you say is your prime suspect?"

"She's his sister," Nancy explained.

"You're kidding," Bess said. She munched on a cherry tomato. "Hey," she teased. "Maybe you've got this whole mystery figured out wrong. Maybe Mick's not behind it. Maybe it's Sondra, trying to help her brother take over the magazine!"

"Yeah," George added. "Then all you'd have to do is find some evidence, get her thrown in jail, and Ned would be yours all over again. And after a bad experience like that, you can bet he'd never step out on you again!"

"It's a great fantasy," Nancy said, laughing. "I'll keep it in mind next time I see them flirting by the water fountain." Then her expression grew serious again. "The thing is, Ned has every reason to be sick of me. I have to admit, I haven't been too nice to him these days. He says I'm more interested in my mystery than in him. And he's right!"

"Nancy, don't say that," Bess scolded. "Ned has to understand that your work is your passion, your life!"

"Right," George agreed. "You put up with him during football season, when he has to be in bed by ten o'clock every night. That's not a real good time for you, but you don't complain."

"It's true," Nancy said, beginning to feel better. "I mean, I *do* complain when Ned's in training, but I don't go out and pick up some cute English major who doesn't have to get up at five in the morning to do push-ups. Of course there was Daryl Grey . . ."

"He's gone and forgotten," Bess insisted. "It doesn't make what Ned's doing right!"

"Yeah," George agreed. "Dating the prime suspect's sister is simply bad taste!"

Nancy had to laugh. It was great having such supportive friends. No matter what she did, George and Bess were always on her side.

The three girls finished their lunches and shared a piece of chocolate cheesecake, amid a lot of joking and laughing.

"So, Bess," said Nancy, "have you heard from Alan Wales lately?"

"My rock star is still on the road," Bess replied, thinking wistfully of the guitarist she'd been dating. "I still don't know what to think of our relationship. It's not over, it's just sort of on hold. Now George, on the other hand . . ."

George blushed.

"What?" asked Nancy.

"She's too embarrassed to say anything, but she's going to see Jon this weekend."

George Fayne didn't fall in love nearly as often as Bess did, but her new boyfriend, a skier, seemed to be very special to her.

Nancy smiled.

She appreciated her friends' company so much that she treated them to lunch. Afterward, George and Bess went off to do some shopping and see an art exhibit before returning to River Heights. Nancy hurried back to *Flash*.

She felt much better. The lunch with George and Bess hadn't solved anything, but the jokes and the gossip had worked wonders for a troubled heart.

Nancy waved hello to Scott and returned to the interns' office. She pulled out the photographs she'd been working on that morning and spread them across the big plank desk.

Mick had asked Nancy to pick out the best pictures from the Danielle Artman shoot. It was harder work than she'd expected because so many of the photos were excellent. Nancy particularly liked one of Danielle kissing a rubber spider.

The work was interesting, and it felt nice to be sitting alone in the quiet office. It almost seemed to Nancy as if everyone else at *Flash* had taken the day off. No problems with Ned. No Sondra Swanson. No potential murderer lurking in the shadows.

Then the sound of a shot rang through the afternoon!

Nancy dashed into the hallway, glancing at her digital watch as she did. It was exactly ten after two. She saw people rushing to the publisher's office and raced after them. Someone threw open the door, and the staff peered into the room, terrified of what they'd find.

Yvonne was standing behind her desk, her ashen face wearing an expression of sheer horror. Then, slowly, her body weakened and she sank to the floor as if dead.

Chapter

Nine

NANCY STARED AGHAST at Yvonne's prone body. Oh, no, she thought. Yvonne is dead! If only I'd called the police after the murder attempt with the spider!

Nancy rushed over to Yvonne, bent down, and gently took her limp wrist to check her pulse. To her intense relief, the publisher's heart was pumping like mad.

"She's alive!" Nancy announced. The staff of *Flash* let out a collective sigh of relief.

Nancy took the publisher's pulse a second time, feeling confused. It was funny that Yvonne's heart was beating so fast. The pulse was supposed to slow down when someone passed out. Nancy shrugged and started massaging Yvonne's shoulders, trying to wake her.

After a minute, Yvonne sat up groggily.

"Yvonne, what happened?" Nancy asked gently. "We heard a gunshot."

Yvonne took a deep breath and pointed to the wall above her desk. A bullet was embedded in the wooden paneling. "I guess I fainted," she mumbled.

"You're okay now, though," Nancy told her. "I'll be right back. I just want to check the fire exit."

Nancy jumped to her feet and ran to the back staircase. The gunman had to have escaped that way because the whole staff had come barreling down the hall in the opposite direction just after the shot was fired. But no one was in the stairway.

Nancy rushed back to the office and found Yvonne starting to explain what had happened. She was lying on the black leather couch, and someone had rolled up a sweater to use as a pillow.

"I was sitting at my desk working," Yvonne began, "when I heard my door being pushed open quietly. I looked up and saw a figure—it looked like a man—wearing dark clothes and a ski mask point a gun at my head! I screamed and the man fired. Then he ran away. That's all," the publisher concluded wearily.

"I think it's time to call the police," Nancy said, looking meaningfully at Yvonne.

"Yes, I guess so," the publisher replied, avoiding Nancy's eyes. "Would you call them, please?"

Nancy picked up the phone on Yvonne's desk

and dialed 911, the police emergency number. "Hello," she said, "there's been a murder attempt at the offices of *Flash* magazine. No one's been hurt, but we need some help."

Nancy gave the police operator her name and *Flash*'s address and hung up. Then she let her eyes wander around the office, trying to discover a clue to the mysterious shooting.

She gazed again at the bullet buried deep in the wall. It was high up, only about two and a half feet from the ceiling. The gunman had missed by a long shot, Nancy thought. The bullet in the paneling was much higher than Yvonne's head would be if she were sitting at her desk. By the look of the hole, Nancy figured the weapon used was probably nothing too powerful. That was surprising, too. Hitmen didn't usually take chances.

Nancy glanced around at the people in the office. David was kneeling by the couch next to Yvonne, holding her hand. Sondra was standing in the back, looking terrified. Ned was there, too, with Scott, Leslie, and a few other interns and staff members. But where was Mick? The art director was nowhere in sight!

The prime suspect was looking more guilty every minute. And if Mick really had shot at Yvonne, that would explain the bad aim and the bad choice of a weapon. As far as Nancy knew, Mick was just an amateur with a grudge.

All at once Nancy realized she could no longer point the finger at anyone other than Mick. The funny thing was, she didn't want him to be the murderer. She would have much preferred that creepy, bad-tempered David be the guilty one. But there was David, with a perfect alibi, while Mick wasn't even around to defend himself.

Nancy dropped into a hardbacked chair by the door to Yvonne's office. She felt overwhelmed. She'd never completely believed Mick was capable of masterminding the threats until just that moment. The art director had only one chance left at that point—to come into the *Flash* offices with an airtight alibi.

Slowly people began drifting out of Yvonne's office. Nancy stayed and talked to Yvonne, trying to get a better description of the masked intruder. How tall was he? Thin or heavyset? Was there anything distinctive about him? But Yvonne's responses were too vague to help.

However, very shortly three police officers showed up—a tall man who introduced himself as Detective Graham, a tough redhaired woman called Officer Bellows, and a refrigerator-sized man named Officer O'Hara who didn't say much, but was very intimidating nonetheless.

Detective Graham and Officer Bellows questioned several staff members. Yvonne had to describe the incident again.

Then Detective Graham took some pictures of Yvonne's office and dug the bullet out of her wall to keep as evidence. After that he went back to the precinct, leaving Officers Bellows and O'Hara behind to keep an eye out for any suspicious activity. Yvonne got ready to leave, too, and David offered to take her home in a taxi. No one in the office seemed ready to do much work. The incident was too bizarre to brush off.

An hour later, Mick sauntered into the office, a camera slung around his neck. "Hey, where've you been?" Leslie called to him. "You missed all the excitement here."

"What's going on?" Mick asked.

"Just a little murder attempt," Scott replied. "Someone tried to shoot Yvonne! We've got no idea who."

Nancy said nothing. *She* had a couple of ideas who, she thought, scrutinizing Mick's face. He was certainly an amazing actor. He really did seem shocked as Leslie described the whole incident.

"You've got to be out of your minds," Mick exclaimed. "All this happened while I was out?" He looked completely amazed.

"What have you been doing?" Nancy asked casually.

"Shooting photographs on the street."

Shooting photographs on the street? Nancy thought. Then he probably has no alibi. No one could vouch for his exact whereabouts at the time of the shooting.

All at once, Mick's serious expression softened into a grin. "Okay, guys, it was a good joke. I admit, I almost believed this insane story. Which one of you crazy geniuses thought it up? You actually fooled the Practical Joke

King!" Mick looked from face to face, but he was the only one laughing. Finally he said, "You're *serious*, aren't you?"

"You can see the bullet hole in the wall if you want proof," Scott said. He stepped out from behind the reception desk. Mick followed him to Yvonne's office.

Nancy definitely didn't want to miss Mick's reaction to the sight of the bullet hole, so *she* followed Scott and Mick. It was a good thing, too, because as she stepped into the hall she heard someone walk into the reception area. "Hi, Brenda. Has anyone told you the big news?" Leslie said.

Great, Nancy thought. Brenda Carlton was not exactly what she needed just then! At least Nancy managed to avoid her again.

Scott opened the door to Yvonne's office. "There it is," he said, motioning to the hole above the desk.

Mick's eyes widened. He was speechless.

Nancy had to admit Mick was doing a great job of seeming flabbergasted. But it had to be an act . . . didn't it? A tiny sliver of doubt crept into Nancy's mind.

"So Yvonne's all right?" Mick asked.

"Luckily," Scott replied.

"And she went home to calm down?"

"Yup."

"Wow, this is so strange," Mick said, his tone incredulous. "I've got to talk to Yvonne. She must be too flipped out for words!"

Nancy watched Mick in amazement. He

seemed so sincere! Suddenly a blood-chilling thought crossed her mind. Maybe Mick really was a split personality! One side of him was wild and funny and concerned with people's feelings. The other side was the crazed killer who could set up the severed head and rubber ax to scare Nancy—or try to shoot his partner and long-time friend in cold blood!

Nancy, Mick, and Scott left Yvonne's office, closing the door behind them. Mick disappeared into his office, while Scott headed toward the reception area.

Nancy started to follow him, then said, "Scott, I'm going to work in the darkroom for a while."

"Okay," Scott answered.

When Scott was out of sight, Nancy tiptoed to Mick's office. As quietly as possible, she turned the doorknob. She pushed open the door without the slightest creak and peeked in, praying to be invisible.

Mick was opening his bottom desk drawer. Nancy had seen him stash his camera there before. All at once a look of utter confusion swept across his handsome face. He reached into the drawer and pulled out a small silver revolver!

Before the rational side of her brain could stop her, Nancy had thrown open the door and was dashing across the room. She threw herself across Mick's desk and tackled the art director.

"Hey!" Mick cried, struggling.

"Drop it, Mick," Nancy advised. "Make it

easy on yourself." She grabbed Mick's arm and twisted with all her might.

"Ow!" Mick yelled, but he kept an iron grip on the revolver, hugging it to his chest.

"I'm sorry to have to do this to you, Mick," Nancy panted. Then she socked the art director as hard as she could in the stomach.

Mick doubled over at the same moment that the gun went off. He fell to the ground, and the gun tumbled out of his hand and onto the shiny wooden floor.

Nancy stared in horror at Mick's prone figure. "Oh no," she whispered. "What have I done?"

"All right," came a shout from the doorway. "Freeze!" Nancy looked up—and into the cocked gun of Officer Bellows. "Nancy Drew," she cried, "you're under arrest!"

Chapter

Ten

"GET YOUR HANDS in the air," Officer Bellows ordered Nancy. "And don't touch that body," she said, indicating Mick, who was immobile on the floor.

Slowly Nancy raised her hands and stepped back from Mick and the gun. She felt helpless and terrified and confused. It had all been an accident, but would that matter to a court of law? She'd been caught red-handed in what looked like murder!

Nancy heard the pounding of feet in the hallway. Officer O'Hara burst into Mick's office, gun in hand. To make things worse, most of the *Flash* staff arrived, too. Ned was there, standing protectively close to Sondra. Suddenly Nancy caught her breath. Brenda Carlton had appeared and was looking at her with a disturbingly triumphant smile on her face. Oh no, Nancy thought, can anything else possibly go wrong?

"Well," Brenda said smugly, "if *this* isn't the scoop of the year! I can just see the headlines. 'Amateur Detective Nancy Drew Murders Top Exec.'"

Nancy felt sick. Brenda had just blown her cover in front of the entire *Flash* staff!

"She's a detective?" Sondra cried. "Then Yvonne *did* hire you to spy on my brother—*and now you've killed him!*" Sondra burst into tears, crying as if she'd never be able to stop.

To Nancy's amazement, Ned put his arm around her, trying to comfort her. The rat! Nancy thought furiously.

"Sondra, it's not like that," Ned said. "Nancy's a good person! This is all a mistake!" But his arm stayed around her shoulders. Nancy felt betrayed and wounded. There she was, being arrested for murder, and her boyfriend was worried about another woman!

Ned's words didn't make any difference to Sondra, who kept crying, or to the rest of the staff, either. They stared at Nancy in stunned and disgusted silence. She felt like a traitor. Brenda's beady eyes glittered happily. She was thoroughly enjoying Nancy's misfortune.

"Okay, Drew," Officer Bellows ordered, "O'Hara's got you covered. Don't try anything funny." Bellows whipped out her handcuffs and snapped them neatly onto Nancy's wrists. Nancy forced back tears. No way was she going to cry in front of all those people.

Suddenly Nancy found her voice. "You've got it all wrong," she cried, struggling against the handcuffs. "*Mick* was the one who tried to kill Yvonne! When I walked into this office, he was pulling that silver revolver out of his bottom desk drawer!"

"*Liar!*" Sondra exclaimed, still sobbing.

"I swear it's true! We were struggling for the gun when it went off! *It wasn't my fault!*" Nancy could feel the tears building up uncontrollably within her.

"Mick's no murderer!" Sondra screamed.

"I saw the proof with my own eyes," Nancy replied vehemently.

"Hey, could you hold it down?" came a voice from the floor. "I've got a horrible headache."

"*Mick!*" cried Sondra. "You're alive!" She burst into a fresh storm of tears. "Thank heavens!"

Nancy breathed a giant sigh of relief.

"My head's killing me," Mick said. "I think I must have hit it on the edge of the desk when I fell."

"All right, Swanson," Officer Bellows said to Mick. "Off the floor. Why don't you tell me *your* side of the story? Drew here's just accused you of trying to kill Yvonne Verdi."

Mick stared at Nancy, a look of hurt betrayal in his blue eyes. "How can you possibly think that?" he asked.

Nancy rolled her eyes. "The gun, Mick, the gun! Don't you remember? You were pulling it out of your desk when I walked in here."

"But it's not mine!" Mick said, turning from Nancy to Officer Bellows. "I've never seen it before in my life. I don't own a gun! The only kind of shooting I know about is photography!"

Officer Bellows stared suspiciously at Mick and Nancy. At last she said, "Looks as though you're *both* going to have to come down to the station." She turned to the others in the room. "The rest of you clear out of here. Detective Graham will be back to question you all."

Slowly, the staff filed out. Brenda threw Nancy a sleazy smile before she left. Soon only Ned and Sondra were left. "Uh, Officer Bellows," Ned said tentatively, "do you think you could take those handcuffs off Nancy? I'll vouch that she's not dangerous, and I think she's pretty uncomfortable with them on."

"Sorry," said Officer Bellows. "Cuffs are standard procedure for bringing in a murder suspect."

"But, Officer, nobody's been murdered," Ned pointed out. "So how about it?"

Officer Bellows blushed, embarrassed. Then, without a word, she set Nancy free. Nancy was filled with grateful relief. For a moment she wanted to throw her arms around Ned and kiss him. But the fact that he had his own arm around Sondra killed the urge right away.

"Let's get moving, you two," Officer Bellows said. Still holding her pistol, she and the silent

O'Hara ushered Nancy and Mick down the hallway, past the gawking staff members and into the elevator. The doors opened and Mick turned to Nancy. "After you, Miss Detective," he said wryly. Ned and Sondra followed, like mourners at a funeral.

Nancy was beginning to have compassion for all the criminals she'd helped to arrest over the years. The public embarrassment of being led off by the cops was horrible! Ned and Sondra hailed a cab and headed toward the police station. Nancy and Mick got into the back of the patrol car while Bellows and O'Hara settled into the front. After a short, miserable ride, they arrived at the precinct.

Officer Bellows had confiscated the revolver as evidence before she'd left *Flash*. As soon as Nancy and Mick had been fingerprinted, she sent the gun to the police lab to be tested against the bullet that Detective Graham had taken out of Yvonne's office wall. Then she let Nancy and Mick make one phone call each.

Luckily, Nancy's father and her attorney were one and the same. It just so happened that Carson Drew was one of the state's finest criminal lawyers. When he heard that Nancy was being held at the police precinct, he promised to be there as fast as he could.

Once Mick had called his lawyer, Officer Bellows and Detective Graham sat down to interrogate their two suspects. The questioning was grueling. The police went over every aspect of the afternoon repeatedly.

The ordeal was made even worse by Ned and Sondra standing around watching the whole thing. Since neither Nancy nor Mick had been accused of a crime yet, they weren't interrogated in private. That meant that Nancy had to watch Ned consoling Sondra, comforting her, trying to calm her fears.

Nancy struggled to keep her mind on Detective Graham's and Officer Bellows's questions, in spite of Ned and Sondra. She had to. If she seemed unsure of her answers, the police would be less likely to believe her side of the story.

When the two officers had finished questioning Nancy, they turned to Mick. To her surprise, he didn't deny anything that had happened. He admitted that the gun had been in his desk, that Nancy hadn't been trying to kill him, that it had all been a crazy mistake. But over and over again he repeated adamantly that the gun had been planted in his desk. "For once," he said, "the joke's on me. And it's not very funny."

Nancy actually felt sorry for Mick. How could he expect the police to accept his silly story when all the evidence was against him? He had no alibi for the afternoon, and any number of motives for wanting to knock off Yvonne.

Nancy wasn't too worried about herself. What could the police accuse her of? Nothing illegal. However, she greeted her father with great relief. He looked so sure of himself and so in control. "Nancy," he said, coming over to kiss his daughter. "Honey, are you all right? I know this isn't pleasant, but just hang on for a little while longer. We'll have you out of here in no time."

Nancy gave her father a huge hug. He'd made it from River Heights in under forty-five minutes. He must have sped all the way here, Nancy thought to herself. Probably the only time he's ever gone above the speed limit in his entire life!

Moments later, the results came back from the lab. The gun and bullet matched.

Officer Bellows turned to Nancy. "Ms. Drew, you're free to leave." Then she faced Mick. "Mr. Swanson," she said solemnly, "you're under arrest for the attempted murder of Yvonne Verdi." Quickly she read him his rights. "Would you come with me? We're going to have to put you in a cell." For the second time that day, the policewoman pulled out her handcuffs.

At first Mick didn't move from his seat. He just blinked uncomprehendingly. Then he jumped up, knocking over his chair. "You think I'm a murderer? Me?" he cried. "But I didn't do it, I swear. That gun isn't mine! *Someone planted it!*"

"You'll have to explain that to the judge and jury," Officer Bellows said calmly.

"And how long will that take?" Mick asked. "A month? Two months? More?"

Suddenly Mick's face turned bright red. Nancy had seen his expression change in the same way on the first day she'd met him—just before he'd smashed Yvonne's vase. He seemed to be losing control of himself.

Grabbing Officer O'Hara's gun out of his holster, Mick shrieked, "You are not going to lock me up for a crime I didn't commit!" He kicked the overturned chair out of his way and made a desperate dash across the room, straight for the precinct door!

Chapter

Eleven

Mick was halfway across the room before anyone reacted to his insane dash toward freedom. And because of his head start, it looked as though he might just make it out of the police station untouched! Then Detective Graham pulled out his pistol. "Stop or I'll shoot!" he cried. But there was no way he could fire with so many people in the room.

Nancy thought fast. She picked up the chair and slid it across the floor, hitting Mick hard in the legs. Mick went down, sprawling just out of reach of the precinct door.

Officer Bellows pounced on the now-prone Mick and snapped her handcuffs on him. "It's a good thing this young woman stopped you," she said. "If you'd escaped, we'd only have tracked you down, and the jury would have been much tougher on you. Now let's go." She pulled Mick to his feet.

"No!" Mick screamed. "I didn't do it!" But Officer Bellows pushed him toward the hallway that held the temporary cells. Soon Mick had disappeared and his cries had died away.

It was then that Nancy noticed Sondra quietly weeping in the corner. But Mick's sister wasn't alone in her misery. Ned was right there with her. Nancy almost swallowed her teeth when she saw him take her in his arms and gently stroke her hair.

"It's all right, Sondra. Don't cry."

"Mick," Sondra sobbed.

Ned continued stroking Sondra. "Don't worry," he told her softly. "If your brother's innocent, we'll get him cleared. Nancy will help us. She's the best detective around!" Ned glanced pleadingly at Nancy.

But Nancy was seething. "I can't believe what I'm hearing," she said through clenched teeth. "Look at you. You're hugging her, and I'm standing right here! You're supposed to care about *me,* Ned. I've been through a lot today. But you don't so much as say a comforting word!"

"Nancy," Ned said, letting go of Sondra and walking hesitantly over to Nancy, "you know it's not like that."

Sondra looked in bewilderment from Ned's face to Nancy's. "You mean you two are going out?" she asked. "Is *he* a spy, too? Is that how he got this job?"

"We *were* going out!" Nancy said. "But I guess he has other plans!" She whirled around and dashed out of the police station. Halting on the steps, she fought back the tears stinging her eyes. "I'm not going to cry," she whispered through gritted teeth.

But Nancy wasn't left alone with her tumultuous thoughts for long. Her father followed her out of the precinct and wrapped a consoling arm around her shoulder.

Nancy threw herself into her father's embrace. "Oh, Dad, how could he do this to me?"

"People sometimes do things they don't mean," Mr. Drew said. "We both know Ned is a fine young man, sensitive and considerate. I think he'll come to his senses, Nancy. Just give him time." But there was really nothing Mr. Drew could say to make his daughter feel better.

"I hate him," Nancy sobbed. "I don't ever want to see him again!"

When Nancy had calmed down, she and her father got into Mr. Drew's silver Cadillac and drove back to River Heights.

For the first half of the ride, Nancy thought she was going to go crazy just imagining Ned and Sondra together. He's probably taking her out for a fancy dinner right now, Nancy thought. And then they'll go dancing at some wild nightclub.

But after a while Nancy couldn't stand imagining those things. She was only making herself more miserable. I've got to stop thinking about them, she decided. I've got to, or I'm going to lose my mind!

It was then that Mick's hysterical words in the police station came back to Nancy. *"You think I'm a murderer? Me? But I didn't do it, I swear. That gun isn't mine! Someone planted it!"* Mick had sounded so surprised at what was happening to him.

With all the evidence against the art director, it seemed as though the case were over, clean and simple. But something was simmering in the back of Nancy's mind.

When Nancy had taken Yvonne's pulse in her office that day, the publisher's heart had been racing. That shouldn't have happened if she had really fainted.

But why would Yvonne fake passing out? Was it possible that she had, in fact, seen the mysterious gunman? Was it someone she wanted to cover for? But why would she cover for someone who was trying to kill her?

Whatever the answer, Nancy was becoming more and more sure that Yvonne was hiding something. Hadn't she had that feeling since her very first day on the case?

Nancy went over that first day in her mind. There'd been that horrible scene with Mick in Yvonne's office and the practical joke with the severed head. After that, Nancy remembered, she'd spent the day developing film for Mick. And she also recalled being surprised at the thoughtful note the art director had written to her about being careful in the darkroom.

Suddenly Nancy caught her breath. Mick's spelling had been worse than a fourth-grader's. He'd confused *your* with *you're* and *their* with *they're*. But in the threatening letters to Yvonne, those words had been spelled correctly! Nancy bit her lip. Mick didn't write those letters, she told herself, suddenly sure. But who did?

Nancy decided to take the train into Chicago the next day and do a little investigating on her own. On a Saturday, no one would be around to get in the way.

Nancy spent a leisurely Saturday morning at home with her father. Ned called once, but Nancy told Hannah Gruen to tell him she wasn't home. She'd tried not to cry then, but a few tears escaped nonetheless.

Nancy caught the eleven-fifteen train into Chicago and was in the lobby of the *Flash* building a few minutes before one. A security guard who looked more asleep than awake asked her to sign a visitor's book. She wrote her name and her time of arrival.

Nancy flipped back a couple of pages and noticed Yvonne's name in the book, too. She'd been up to the office late Thursday night. What a workaholic, Nancy thought.

Once Nancy had signed the book, the guard motioned her toward the elevators. It bothered her that he hadn't asked for her I.D. Security certainly was lax!

Nancy rode up to the *Flash* offices. She had

made a point of watching Scott activate and deactivate the security system a few times, so she knew just how it worked. All she had to do was push the right coded numbers and the alarm was deactivated. Then Nancy used her credit card to pick the lock. In less than five minutes she had the *Flash* offices completely to herself.

Nancy decided to begin her search in Mick's office. She picked the lock on his door and stepped inside. It looked the same as always, except that Mick's camera was sitting on his desk. Nancy remembered that he'd left it there Friday afternoon, just before she'd come in and clobbered him.

Nancy picked up the expensive Nikon camera. It was still loaded. Well, she thought, I might as well get this film developed and see what it has to show. She rewound the film, opened the back of the camera, and emptied out the finished roll.

Nancy hurried down the hall to the darkroom. She knew she was taking a big liberty in developing Mick's photos without his knowledge, but since she was only doing it in order to clear him of a crime, she figured she was justified.

Nancy let herself into the darkroom and quickly set up the chemicals she'd need to turn the negatives into full-color photos. She worked hard, and soon she had a print of each picture ready.

Nancy sat down with the wet prints and began

scrutinizing them for clues. Most of the shots were pretty arty, contrasting light and shadow or picking up odd mixtures of people in the same shot. The work was very different from the commercial portraits Mick took for *Flash*. He was clearly talented at both types of photography.

Still, none of the pictures helped Nancy much. But they have to! Nancy thought in frustration. I've got nothing else to go on! She redoubled her efforts, checking each photo even more closely.

Thoughtfully, Nancy picked up a picture showing a newspaper stand. There was no doubt that Mick had a special touch with a camera. The newsstand looked so clear. Nancy could actually see Friday's date on the front of one of the papers, and the words on the nearby street sign. Even the shadows were clear.

Suddenly Nancy realized that the photo might be the clue she was looking for! It could be just the thing needed to establish an alibi for Mick. Nancy checked every detail of the picture. It was all there—the street signs to indicate place, the newspapers to show the date. Now if she could just establish the time the picture had been taken, Mick would have an airtight alibi!

Mick had said he'd been shooting the film at the same time that Yvonne had been attacked. If so, the shadows would prove it—since shadows change length according to how high in the sky the sun is. A two o'clock shadow was the same length on Friday as it was on Saturday.

Nancy glanced at her digital wristwatch. It showed a quarter of two, a little before the time the gunman had invaded the *Flash* studio on Friday. If she hopped into a taxi, she could be at the newsstand in twenty minutes. Nancy grabbed the picture and dashed out of the office, being careful to reset the alarm before she left.

It wasn't hard to find the newsstand. It was the only one at the intersection shown on the street sign. Nancy pulled the photo from her bag as she got out of the taxi and slammed the door. She checked the time again. Five after two. Perfect! Nancy had heard Yvonne scream at ten after.

The photo showed that the shadow of the signpost just reached the edge of the newsstand. The picture was so clear there could be no mistake. Nancy took a careful look at the real street sign and newsstand. Sure enough, the shadows matched!

Nancy let out a triumphant cry. She'd cleared Mick! He'd been far from *Flash* at two o'clock Friday afternoon. He couldn't possibly have taken the photo, then rushed back to shoot Yvonne. Besides, Mick had never tried to use the picture as an alibi. That meant there was no reason for it to be a fake.

So, Nancy told herself, the case isn't over after all. But what did the new development mean? Obviously, the culprit was trying to frame Mick by planting the gun in his desk, but who *was* the culprit? David? Someone else working for MediaCorp? Or just a person who hated Yvonne and Mick?

Nancy knew that she was facing what was the least favorite part of a mystery for her—waiting for the criminal's next move. Meanwhile, a potential killer was on the loose. And when it became known that Nancy had cleared Mick, the criminal just might turn his wrath upon Nancy herself!

Chapter
Twelve

Nancy, when are you going to stop dragging into Chicago on these commuter trains and start driving your gorgeous blue Mustang again?" Bess Marvin demanded. "It's such a bummer having to take this smelly old train."

"When they turn the Sears Building into the world's tallest garage," Nancy said with a smile. "Really, you wouldn't believe how hard it is to find parking in the city."

"Oh," Bess said dreamily, "but there's nothing like cruising down the parkway in that Mustang of yours, the wind blowing through our hair, the sun shining . . ."

"Please, Bess," George said sarcastically. "You sound like a car commercial!" Nancy giggled.

"Aha," George cried, "did I detect a laugh coming from our sad and serious Ms. Drew? I knew your funnybone wasn't broken."

Nancy flashed her friends an apologetic smile. "I'm sorry, you guys. I know I'm not being much fun. But this thing with Ned—"

"Stop right there. Don't say another word," George told Nancy. "We know you're miserable, and we know you probably need a little moral support from your best friends. Why do you think we decided to go into town today? It wasn't because Bess *really* needs that black suede dress."

"I do too need it," Bess protested, "and that stupid store wouldn't take an out-of-town check!"

Nancy smiled again. "It doesn't matter. I'm just glad to have you two around."

Nancy leaned back in her seat and listened to the rhythmic clatter of the train. She was dreading going in to *Flash*. Things were bound to be volatile, for a number of reasons. For starters, Mick would be back at work. Nancy had gone down to the police station with the newsstand photograph on Saturday and explained everything to Detective Graham. Mick had been out of jail within fifteen minutes. But how would the rest of the staff react to him? How would Yvonne behave? Not normally, that was certain.

Also, everyone at *Flash* knew Nancy was a detective, and probably thought she was

Yvonne's stool pigeon. Nancy was sure she'd be getting the cold shoulder from a lot of people she'd thought were her friends.

Nancy was going to have to see Ned and Sondra, too. She'd managed to avoid Ned's calls all weekend, but he'd left a message for her on Sunday. He'd thanked her for getting Mick out of prison and said that he intended to go back to *Flash* on Monday as an intern. After all, Brenda hadn't blown *his* cover, except with Sondra. He promised to let Nancy know about anything strange that he saw. He'd also said he wanted to see her and hoped they could work things out.

Fat chance, Nancy said to herself.

Nancy was definitely not thrilled about the day's prospects. But having Bess and George to talk to on the train made it all a little better. "I don't know what I'm going to do," Nancy told her friends. "I think I'm going to melt into the ground when I see Ned. Either that or punch him out."

"He's really acting like a creep," Bess agreed.

"But how come?" George wondered. "I mean, Ned's always been totally crazy about you. He's never so much as *looked* at another girl. So why now?"

Nancy sighed. "I think I might be partly to blame. Ned was feeling unappreciated. He said I was always busy working and never had time for him. I did treat our vacation pretty lightly.

But Ned's been my boyfriend for *years.* And—and I miss him." Suddenly Nancy felt as if she were about to cry.

"Hey, it's okay," George said softly. "Look, either Ned will regain his senses and come back to you, or he's a real jerk and not worth the tears."

"Right," Bess said.

Nancy stared morosely at the dirty train floor. It was a no-win situation. Either she pretended she hated Ned and felt awful or admitted she loved him and felt even worse!

When they reached the city, Nancy kissed her friends goodbye. "Do you want to meet at the end of the day and go back to River Heights together?" Bess asked.

"I wish I could," Nancy said, "but I have no idea when I'm going to be done at *Flash,* so I'll have to pass. I'll see you at home."

"Okay. Good luck," Bess said, giving Nancy an extra hug.

"And be careful today," George advised.

Wow, Nancy thought as she caught the downtown subway, I've got some really great friends —no matter how rotten my boyfriend is!

But as Nancy neared the *Flash* building she found her fears about Ned gradually being replaced by worries about the case. Someone in that office was a potential killer. The murderer might even be after *her* now. And she was sure no one at *Flash* was going to be too eager to help her find more information at that point.

Nancy felt like a first-time parachuter. She

was about to step into a huge void, and she had no idea what to expect. All she could do was take the leap and hope the parachute worked!

Nancy could feel the change in atmosphere at *Flash* as soon as she stepped into the reception area. Two reporters who were walking by stopped to stare rudely at her. Nancy sighed. Then, trying to make everything seem as normal as possible, she put a smile on her face and called, "Hey, Scott, how's it going?" as she'd done each morning.

"What are you doing here?" Scott replied shortly.

"I—" Scott's coldness stopped Nancy short. She hadn't expected that from *him*. She steeled herself. "I work here. I'm investigating an attempted murder, trying to make sure Yvonne doesn't get killed." Then she added more gently, "Is that so bad?"

Scott stared at his blank computer screen in embarrassment. Finally he mumbled, "That's not the problem. The problem is what you've been reporting to Yvonne. Some of the things I've said about her haven't been too flattering— and I don't want to lose my job."

Nancy sighed. "I haven't been ratting on the people who work here, Scott. That's not what I was hired to do."

"I wish I could believe that," Scott answered. He glanced at Nancy, and in that instant she detected an unmistakable look of fear. Wow, he is really scared, Nancy thought. Then she began to wonder how the others would react. She wanted to wring Brenda Carlton's neck! Once again, she'd ruined everything.

"Mick wants to see you," Scott told Nancy. "He's in the studio doing a shoot. Yvonne wants to see you, too, in her office."

"Thanks," Nancy said, turning to leave.

"Oh, and Sondra left you this." Scott handed Nancy a small, folded piece of paper.

Nancy stepped away from the reception desk, frowning. What does she want? she wondered. She unfolded the paper and read the note:

Dear Nancy,
   How can I ever thank you for what you've done for Mick? I feel really bad about the horrible things I said to you. Do you think we can straighten things out?

Your friend (I hope),
Sondra

Nancy looked at the note angrily, then crumpled it up and threw it in a nearby wastepaper basket. Sondra hadn't said a single word about Ned!

Nancy walked slowly toward the studio. She knew a lot of the staff would be at the shoot—and judging by Scott's reaction to her, they probably wouldn't be too friendly. Well, she would have to face them at some point. It might as well be now.

When Nancy stepped into the studio she immediately saw Sondra and Ned and purposely avoided making eye contact with either of them. As for the others, no one so much as said hello to Nancy until Mick spotted her.

"Nancy!" he cried. He left his camera and ran over to her, throwing his arms around her in a huge, friendly hug.

Mick's reaction was as uncomfortable for Nancy as the lack of reaction from everyone else. After all, Nancy and Mick hadn't exactly been big buddies before she'd sprung him from jail. Suddenly everything at *Flash* was topsy-turvy. Nancy's friends had deserted her. And the people she hadn't really trusted, like Mick and Sondra, were the only ones being civil to her.

"Nancy," Mick was saying as he casually draped his arm around her shoulder, "I asked you to come here so I could thank you for clearing me. I certainly didn't do anything to deserve your help. I'm really grateful."

Nancy smiled. "Well, I couldn't let an innocent man sit in jail, could I?"

"I'm going to make it up to you somehow," Mick said intently. "I'm not sure how right now, but I will."

"I don't expect any kind of reward," Nancy said. But she had to admit, after all the flak she was getting from other people in the office, that it did feel good to have at least one full-fledged fan.

"You're a good kid," Mick said. He planted a brotherly kiss on Nancy's cheek. "I've got to get back to work now, but we'll talk later, okay?"

"Okay," Nancy said, heading for the door. She shot a glance at Ned before she left. He was gazing at her soulfully. But Nancy wasn't about to give him a break. She tossed her head haughtily and stepped out of the studio.

Forcing a brave smile onto her face, Nancy walked to Yvonne's office.

I wonder how Yvonne's reacting to all this, Nancy thought. She knocked on her door.

"Who's there?"

"It's me, Nancy."

"Door's open. Come in."

"Hi," Nancy said, opening the door and stepping into the publisher's office. She gave Yvonne a friendly smile and closed the door behind her.

But Yvonne wasn't smiling. In fact, her expression was decidedly angry. "Just exactly what are you trying to do?" she burst out.

"I—I don't understand," Nancy said, confused.

"Oh, you don't?" the publisher said sarcastically. "Then let me spell it out for you. I hired you to stop the person who's trying to kill me—"

"And that's just what I'm trying to do," Nancy said, attempting another smile. Yvonne hadn't asked her to sit down, and she felt awkward standing in front of her.

But Yvonne wasn't taking any peace offerings. "Mick's trying to kill me," she practically screamed, "and the detective *I* hired gets him out of jail so he can finish the job!"

"Yvonne, you've got it all wrong," Nancy cried. "It's not Mick! I have proof of that!" She paused. "I don't know how to tell you this, but I think it might be David!"

"David!" Yvonne snorted. "What a ridiculous idea. David loves me—and Mick owns the murder weapon."

"No, he doesn't," Nancy said. "That gun was planted in Mick's desk. I know for certain that he wasn't anywhere near the *Flash* building when that shot was fired. Someone's trying to frame him, and I think it might be David. Don't you know that he works for MediaCorp? They've sent him checks!"

For a moment, Yvonne just stared at Nancy. Then she said, "If this is a joke, it's a very bad one. I really don't know what to say except—Nancy Drew, you're fired!"

Chapter

Thirteen

Wow, I FEEL like someone in one of your magazine articles," Nancy exclaimed to Mick. She spread the skirt of her gold silk dress across the seat of the limousine and leaned back against the plush leather cushion.

"Do you want something to drink?" Mick asked, motioning to the car bar. "Sprite, Coke?"

"I'll take a Coke, thanks," Nancy said, feeling very luxurious. "Gosh, I'm so excited. The Maggie Awards! I've heard about them for years, and watched them on TV, but now I'm actually going to *be* there to see it all happen!"

"Imagine how *I* feel," Mick said, handing Nancy her soda and taking a sip of his own drink. "I've known about the Maggies for years, too. Who would have guessed that my magazine would eventually be nominated for one?"

"Actually, my friend Bess would have," Nancy said with a laugh. "She's been saying *Flash* should win the best teen magazine award for months now." Nancy stared out the window as the limo cruised through the streets of Chicago from Mick's fancy apartment to the Palace nightclub, where the Maggie ceremony would be held.

"Well, we haven't won yet," Mick said, trying to check his excitement. "We've only been nominated. We've got to beat out four other magazines to get the award." He turned to Nancy and smiled. "By the way, you look great."

Nancy's flowing, full-length gold silk dress with long split sleeves showed off her figure beautifully. It was the perfect color to complement her shiny reddish blond hair. She'd completed the outfit with simple gold jewelry, gold sandals, and a gold clutch. She knew she looked good. And she needed to! Mick had told her Ned was going to be at the ceremony, too—with Sondra.

"Thank you, Mick," Nancy said, "but there's no way I could compare with you!" She looked at the art director and smiled. He was wearing beautifully cut tails with a white silk shirt and a black bow tie. Since it was impossible for Mick to wear anything traditional, the tails were made of soft black leather.

Mick smiled, then bit his lip. "Got to look my

best, just in case *Flash* does win and I have to go up there in front of the hottest people in the business to accept the award." He shot a worried glance at Nancy. "Anyway," he went on, "no matter what happens tonight, I'm glad I could share the evening with you. You've done so much for me."

"I know," Nancy said, giggling. "You definitely were not too thrilled about spending time in jail. Hey, I'm thankful for your invitation to the Maggies. I've been feeling a little like a social outcast these days."

"It's kind of crazy the way everyone at the office turned against you," Mick said sympathetically. "I guess they're all a little scared of Yvonne. When they found out you were working for her—well, they just wanted to stay away from you."

"As of one week ago, I'm *not* working for her," Nancy said, tapping her fingers on the armrest. "I just don't understand. How could Yvonne fire me when I'm only trying to protect her? And how can she ignore the facts? It's weird!"

"Well, I'm glad you're still working on it," Mick said. "I need to find out who tried to frame me."

"It's not really me—it's Ned," Nancy said. "He might make me furious at him, but he is a good detective. And since only you, Sondra, and Yvonne know who he really is . . ."

"You know, Yvonne tried to fire him, too.

But I told her I liked his work." Mick grinned. "I just didn't tell her it was his detective work I liked."

Nancy finished her soda. "One way or another, we're going to get concrete proof against whoever's behind these threats, and I'm going to make sure Yvonne stays alive long enough to see that I'm right!"

Mick laughed. "You're a fighter, Nancy. You're the most determined person I've ever met." He glanced out the window. "Here we are."

The limo pulled up in front of what in the daytime probably looked like an old abandoned theater. But at the moment, it was bustling with activity. As Nancy and Mick got out of the car, cameras started clicking in a blinding series of flashes. "That's Mick Swanson," Nancy heard someone saying, "but who's the gorgeous woman he's with?"

Nancy beamed. She felt like a real celebrity. She and Mick were ushered quickly into the club. The inside was nothing at all like its unkempt outside. A long red carpet welcomed the guests as if they were royalty, and the Palace glittered with lights. Huge vases of flowers lined the wide hallway leading to the main room. A tall woman in a floor-length gown whisked their coats away.

Nancy walked with Mick into the award room feeling as though she owned the place. But her confidence sank down to the hem of her silk dress as soon as she saw Ned and Sondra standing cozily together in a spot she and Mick would have to pass to find seats.

Sondra wore a stunning green off-the-shoulder evening gown. And Ned looked so handsome that Nancy could barely stand it. He was always a killer in a formal suit.

Nancy felt like running off to the bathroom and stalling for time, but she knew that would be silly. Steeling herself, she walked right up to Ned and Sondra, Mick following closely behind. "Hi," she said, trying to sound pleasant, but not too pleasant. It was hard to smile when your heart felt as if it had been split open with a meat cleaver.

"Nancy!" Sondra cried. "I'm so glad you're here. You look fabulous."

"Thanks," Nancy replied tightly.

"Hello, Nancy," Ned said, giving her an intense look. "I've been trying to call you recently but you're never home."

"Yes, I've been busy," Nancy said coolly. "I think I'm going to be busy for a long time."

Meanwhile, Mick had given his sister a hug and a kiss. "Hey, Ned," he said. The two young men shook hands. After that, the foursome stood around uncomfortably for a moment. Finally Mick said, "Well, Nancy, should we go find seats?"

"Sure," Nancy agreed. There was nothing she wanted more than to get away from Ned and Sondra.

"We'll see you at the party after the awards," Sondra told them.

Nancy and Mick found seats in the middle of the audience. "That wasn't so bad, was it?" Mick asked Nancy sympathetically.

"No, but I'm hoping the rest of the evening will be better," Nancy answered, smiling at Mick.

"We should talk about that sometime," Mick told Nancy.

"What's to say?" Nancy asked.

"*Lots,*" Mick replied emphatically. "I'm not sure you really understand what's going on between those two."

"The less I know, the better," Nancy said.

"Not necessarily," Mick returned. "Anyway, this is not the time or the place to go into a heavy discussion, so we'll have to do it later."

"Okay, that's fine," Nancy said.

She turned away and looked around the audience to see if she knew anyone. She recognized a few models and other celebrities, all wearing their glitziest. Yvonne, she saw, was sitting in front, close to the stage. She was wearing a classic black gown, and her hair was pulled softly away from her face. What do you know? Nancy thought. Yvonne actually wore something other than a business suit.

David was sitting next to Yvonne, looking as cold and untrustworthy as ever. Nancy just couldn't understand what Yvonne saw in him.

Nancy and Mick settled into their seats and soon the Maggie ceremony began. Nancy found all the preliminary awards very boring, since she didn't know anything about the magazine business. But there was still plenty for her to look at—the great clothes, for instance.

Finally, the master of ceremonies announced the best teen magazine award. "Here goes," Nancy whispered. "I'm crossing all my fingers and all my toes for you."

"Me, too," Mick whispered back.

"The competition's been tough this year," the M.C. said, "but our judges came to a unanimous decision despite that. The envelope, please . . ." Nancy held her breath as the M.C. took the envelope and ripped it open. "And the winner is . . . *Flash* magazine. Congratulations, Yvonne Verdi and Mick Swanson!"

"We did it!" Mick cried excitedly to Nancy. "We actually did it!" He gave Nancy a big bear hug.

Nancy hugged Mick back. "Fantastic! You and *Flash* deserve it!"

Mick squeezed his way to the end of their row and walked up to the stage. Nancy could tell he was trying to look suave, but his happiness came through clearly in the bounciness of his stride.

Mick met Yvonne at the steps to the stage, and they walked up together and crossed the stage. When they reached the podium, Mick turned and smiled happily at Yvonne.

At that moment, there was a terrific splintering sound. One of the heavy lights hanging from the ceiling broke loose and came crashing down —headed straight for Mick and Yvonne!

Chapter

Fourteen

HEY, MICK, I brought you something," Nancy told the bandaged and unmoving figure in the bed.

"Not more flowers, I hope," Mick said. "People have given me so many I'm beginning to think I'm in a funeral home instead of a hospital."

"Well, a beautiful spring Thursday would probably be a nice day to be buried on," Nancy joked. "Anyway, thank goodness you aren't going to be." She dropped into a little chair by Mick's bedside. "That light could have finished you off with no trouble. If it had hit you squarely instead of just grazing you, that would have been the end. Thank goodness Yvonne jumped out of the way in time."

"Yeah, I guess I was lucky," Mick said with a

laugh. "All I got was a dislocated shoulder, a broken leg, five stitches in my arm, and assorted cuts and bruises. That's the kind of luck you wish on your worst enemy!"

"Speaking of enemies," Nancy said casually, "do you have any, Mick?"

Mick adjusted himself uncomfortably in the bed. "Hey, what kind of a question is that? And what happened to the present you brought me?"

"Okay," Nancy said, laughing. "Present first. Questions later. Deal?"

"Deal."

Nancy took a silver-wrapped box from her shoulder bag and handed it to Mick. "Get well soon," she said. "Your cameras miss you."

"Uh, do you think you could open that for me? I'm kind of incapacitated here."

"Of course." Nancy tore away the silver foil and took the top off the box. Inside was a remote control dune buggy, perfect for Mick since it was painted with zebra stripes. "It reminded me of those shoes you have," Nancy told him, "so I just had to buy it."

"I *love* it," Mick said. "It's going to be the prize of my collection when I get back to the office. Put it on the floor."

Nancy set the dune buggy down beside Mick and handed him the remote control. Mick had a great time making it do tricks for a few minutes. Pressing the buttons was about the only activity he could do easily, because of his bandages and casts.

"So, Nancy, why the question about enemies?" he asked finally, dropping the remote control onto the bed.

Nancy sighed. "I hate to tell you this, but the police found out that the light didn't fall by accident. The wire holding it in place had been cut—and by a very ingenious device. An ax had been rigged up to a remote control—"

"Oh, no," Mick groaned. "Another murder attempt against Yvonne! You don't still suspect me, do you?"

"No. That photo of the newsstand clears you. Besides, half the *Flash* staff saw the stunt you pulled on me and the other half heard about it. Anyone could have used the same trick at the Maggies."

"Whew," Mick said. "I'm glad the killer didn't get Yvonne. She's not as bad as I sometimes make her out to be."

"Yes, the killer messed up again," Nancy told Mick, "but maybe the murderer wasn't as far off the mark as we think! You see, everyone assumes the 'accident' was meant for Yvonne and not you because there have already been two other attempts on her life. But what if that light was meant to get you both?"

"But, Nancy," said Mick with a gasp, "why?"

Nancy leaned forward and rested her hand on Mick's good arm. "Here's what I think. Those other attempts were meant to kill Yvonne and discredit you at the same time. So our killer is out to get you, too."

"That's true," Mick said slowly.

"Well," Nancy continued, "once I cleared you, the creep could no longer do that. So now he has to kill you *and* Yvonne in order to get you both out of the way!"

Mick was silent for a moment. "That's really frightening," he said at last. "But who's doing it, Nancy? And why?"

"I'm not sure," Nancy said thoughtfully, "but I have a few good ideas. It's highly possible that MediaCorp's behind the whole thing. By getting rid of *Flash*'s owners, they'd be able to buy the magazine cheaply and without any trouble."

"Incredible!" Mick cried.

"If it *is* MediaCorp, I'd lay bets that David's doing the dirty work. He's on their payroll, you know. I found the evidence in his office. At this point, it's all just speculation," Nancy said more realistically, "but it's a theory I want to investigate further."

"It's a great theory!" Mick exclaimed. "Because other than MediaCorp, I don't think I have any enemies. At least none who hates me enough to try to kill me!"

"Then you think MediaCorp would actually go as far as murder to get something they want?"

"I'm not sure, but it's possible. I told Yvonne that MediaCorp would never give her the price she was asking for *Flash*. Even if I agreed to sell."

"But, Mick," Nancy said, "Yvonne told me she's not planning to sell at *any* price."

"That's what she *says*. Believe me, Nancy, she has her price. Why would I lie to you?"

"Why would *Yvonne* lie?" she said.

"I can't answer that," Mick said.

"Neither can I. Anyway, I'm hoping you'll be able to give me a few leads on what happened at the Maggies. Did you see anything odd? Anyone suspicious in the audience?"

Mick thought for a moment. "I can't remember anything unusual. But to tell you the truth, I was too excited to notice very much that night. It was like a fantasy come true—and who looks for flaws in the middle of a living fantasy?" Mick sighed, remembering the evening. "And to think I never got to accept my award. Now that is a real tragedy!"

Nancy laughed. "Well, you certainly made the biggest splash in the history of the Maggie ceremonies! I'm just glad you're all right." Nancy decided to let the questioning go. Clearly, Mick wasn't going to be able to help her much.

"How are you keeping yourself occupied?" she asked.

"Doing a lot of reading," Mick told her. "Yvonne was really sweet. She brought over a whole bunch of mystery novels for me." He pointed to a stack of paperbacks piled on his night table.

"That was thoughtful of her," Nancy mused.

"Yeah. This accident has actually made her want to be civil—even nice—to me."

"Are any of the books any good? Yvonne

didn't seem very interested in mysteries when I first met her. I wouldn't suppose she'd know the best writers."

"Are you kidding?" Mick said incredulously. "Yvonne's the biggest mystery fanatic south of Alaska! She probably knows more about them than you or I do! She even *wrote* a few after she got out of college. I've read them. Real thrillers."

Nancy gasped. "And I bet I can guess her pen name. She's not, by any chance, Ivan Green, is she?"

"Brilliant deduction, Detective Drew," Mick said with a laugh. "Ivan, which sounds like Yvonne, and Green, which is English for the Italian word *verdi*, her last name."

Nancy suddenly glanced at her watch. "Oh, look, it's almost five o'clock!" she exclaimed with fake surprise. "I promised my father I'd meet him for dinner at quarter after, so I'd better be running." Nancy leaned down to kiss Mick's cheek.

"Well, thanks for coming, Nancy. You've definitely broken the monotony of hospital life. And I love the dune buggy. It's kind of like a pet puppy."

"I'm glad. I'll come visit you again soon." Nancy grinned at Mick, but her smile disappeared the moment she stepped out of his room. She was thinking hard. She had a lot of work ahead of her, and she knew she wouldn't be able to do it all alone. But who could she ask for help? Usually she called Bess or George, but they were in River Heights. Too far away. Ned? After everything that had happened between them, could she still call him?

Nancy gave an exasperated sigh. I'll have to, she decided, no matter how much pride is at stake.

Nancy hurried to the hospital cafeteria and found a telephone. Not stopping for a moment, she pushed seven numbers.

The phone rang once before Scott's voice said, "Hello, *Flash* magazine."

"Yes, I'd like to speak to Ned Nickerson," Nancy said, trying not to sound like herself.

"Hold one moment," Scott said. He hadn't recognized her voice.

The next voice Nancy heard was Ned's. "Hello?" he said.

"Hi, Ned, this is Nancy. Are you alone?"

"Oh, wow, I'm so glad you finally called!" Ned exclaimed happily. "I've missed you so much. When can we get together and talk this thing out?"

"Hold on. I'm not calling to make up, and I don't want to hear the sordid details of your relationship with Sondra."

"What sordid details?" Ned cried. "All we did was—"

"I don't care." Nancy cut Ned off. "I need to talk to you about something much more important."

"More important than us, Nancy? I don't think that exists."

"Great. Butter me up, Ned Nickerson. Give

me the whole dairy farm! It still doesn't excuse what you've done to me—to us!"

Ned sighed. "Please, let's not fight again."

"Right. I don't have time for it. We've got to meet. Stay at *Flash*. I'll be over there as fast as it takes me to catch a taxi downtown."

"What's up?" Ned asked.

"I've solved the mystery!" Nancy announced. Suddenly she was full of energy and excitement again.

"And you need my help to catch the person who's responsible, right?"

"Not person—people," Nancy told Ned.

"You mean there's more than one?" Ned said, incredulous.

"Yup, there are two! And you'll never guess who!"

Chapter
Fifteen

Two, Nancy? Who?" asked Ned.

"Well, one of them's David Bower."

"That's no big surprise," Ned said. "What about the second?"

Nancy took a deep breath. "You're not going to believe this, but—Yvonne Verdi!"

"*Yvonne?* Nancy, that's impossible. Yvonne's the one they're trying to kill!"

"Nope, Yvonne's the one they're trying to make it *seem* as though they're trying to kill. But really, Mick's been the target of this scheme all along. I'll explain the whole thing later. Just be at *Flash* when I get there."

"Okay, Nancy. I love—" But she had already hung up the telephone.

Nancy dashed out of the hospital. She found a taxi right away and within seconds was shooting downtown, the driver dodging bikers and pedestrians. I hope Yvonne and David haven't gone home yet. I hope I haven't missed them! she thought.

The ride to *Flash* took only fifteen minutes, but it felt like hours to Nancy. Wrapping up a mystery and catching the criminals was always hard, but this time an extra complication was going to make it even tougher.

Oh, Ned, Nancy cried to herself, why did you have to leave me? Then her anger flared. How dare you leave me! And how am I ever going to keep my mind on my plan when I feel like this? Nancy nibbled nervously on the nail of her index finger.

Nancy forced herself to think of the plan she was about to carry out—a plan which, if it worked, was going to nab her two attempted murderers. She'd have to play it cool and time things perfectly with Ned. Otherwise there was a good chance *she* would be the next victim!

Suddenly Nancy called to the taxi driver, "Hey, stop here, in front of this Woolworth's. Keep the meter running. I'll be back in two minutes, okay?"

"Fine with me," the driver said, pulling up in front of the store.

Nancy jumped out of the car and hurried into the store. She spent less than five minutes inside. When she ran back out she was clutching a small brown paper bag. "I think I just broke the shopper's speed record," she commented to the driver as she jumped into the taxi. As he peeled away from the curb, she stuffed the package into her shoulder bag.

It didn't take long to reach the *Flash* building. Nancy paid the driver and tumbled out of the car. Once again she rode the elevator upstairs. She glanced at her watch. It was just after five-thirty. Good, she thought. She was sure that at least one of the crooks was still there and the rest of the staff was probably gone, so they wouldn't mess anything up.

The elevator doors opened on the sixteenth floor, and Nancy stepped out. There was Ned— but he wasn't alone! A yellow-haired figure stood next to him.

Nancy marched angrily over to Ned. She was seething but she hid her feelings as best she could. "Hello," she said evenly.

"Sondra insisted on coming," Ned told Nancy.

"I want to help," Sondra explained. "It's the least I can do for the girl who saved my brother." She gave Nancy a smile full of warmth and hope.

Nancy was silent.

"Nancy," Ned said, moving closer to her, "I told you, it's not the way you think it is. You're supposed to be a detective. Please don't jump to conclusions before you have all the facts!"

Suddenly Sondra cut in. "Hold it, you two. You both sound ridiculous. Why don't you try to communicate for real? First thing, Ned, is that you have to be more understanding of Nancy. She probably has good reason to feel a little jealous. But, Nancy, you haven't let Ned explain a word! How's he supposed to get through to you? I'm going to have to take charge here, or we'll never catch the crooks we came for!"

Sondra looked from Nancy to Ned and back. "Good. Now that you've both shut up long enough to listen, I'm going to set you two straight. Nancy, I didn't steal your boyfriend, no matter what you think. I'll admit at first I was really attracted to Ned. But that was before I found out you two'd been going out for so long. Ned's really helped me recently, at a time when everything seemed to be going wrong. I appreciate it," Sondra said simply. "He's been a good friend to me, a close friend—and that's all!

"But, Ned," Sondra continued, "I think you used me to get back at Nancy a little. You were mad at her for not spending enough time with you, and the fact that she got so jealous did wonders for your ego. Come on, you know it's true!"

"I refuse to admit a thing," Ned said, but a tiny smile played at the corners of his lips.

"It's clear to me that you two love each other. But to tell you the truth, I don't care about any of this," Sondra said, "at least not right now. Because we've got some serious detective work to do. The three of us are just going to have to make up. Got it?"

Nancy glanced at Sondra out of the corner of her eye. She had to admit Sondra knew how to get things done. If it had been up to me and Ned, the crooks would have gotten halfway to Acapulco before we even stopped fighting, Nancy said to herself. Nancy couldn't help but admire Sondra. She'd really be okay—if only she'd stay away from Ned!

"All right," Nancy said at last. "Are Yvonne and David still here?"

"Yvonne is," Ned answered. "David went home an hour ago."

"That's fine. Once we've gotten a confession out of Yvonne, David will be easy to nab."

"So where do we start?" Sondra wanted to know.

"In the darkroom, across from Yvonne's office. You two stay there. I'll be with Yvonne. Give me fifteen minutes, then come out and make sure I'm okay." Nancy reached into her shoulder bag. "Here, Ned, I have something to give you." Then she pulled out a small pistol. She was holding it by the barrel.

"Nancy!" Ned exclaimed. "What are you doing with that thing? You've never even touched one before, and neither have I! And what's more, I don't intend to start now. Throw it away!"

Nancy giggled. "Good, I'm glad it's so convincing. Ned, it's a water pistol, and one of the most realistic I've ever seen. I bought it at Woolworth's on the way over here. If I really do get in trouble with Yvonne, running into her office and yelling 'Boo' isn't going to help. But a gun—or what she thinks is a gun—will!"

Sondra laughed. "Catching a crook with a toy gun! My brother would really appreciate this!"

Ned frowned, but pocketed the water pistol. "Nancy," he said, "I think you have a few disconnected wires."

"It's called improvising," Nancy said with a smile. "You guys ready?"

"Sure, I've got my plastic gun, haven't I?" Ned joked. Then his expression changed to one of concern. "Nancy, be careful."

"I will. Don't worry. Now come on."

Nancy, Ned, and Sondra sneaked quietly down the corridor to the darkroom off of Mick's office. "How are we going to get in? It's locked," Sondra whispered.

Nancy pulled out her credit card and gave Sondra a grin. In half a minute the door was open. "Okay, you two. Remember, fifteen minutes, just long enough for me to get the confession on tape. You're my life insurance!"

Ned and Sondra stepped into the darkroom and Nancy closed the door gently. Then she reached into her shoulder bag and pushed the record button on her tiny portable tapedeck. Walking across the hallway, she knocked softly on Yvonne's office door. There was no answer, even after she knocked a second time.

Finally Nancy pushed open the door. The publisher wasn't there. Well, I'll just have to wait for her, Nancy decided. She knew Yvonne hadn't left for the day because her door was unlocked.

Nancy closed the door and leaned thoughtfully against the leather couch. So Yvonne had turned out to be just as selfish and egotistical as she'd seemed to Nancy that first day. However, she also had an evil streak that Nancy hadn't counted on. She hadn't really cared about the magazine at all, just her own success and her wallet. She'd even been willing to kill off Mick, an old friend, when he'd gotten in the way.

Nancy started pacing the room. Where was Yvonne, anyway? Nancy had told Ned and Sondra to appear in fifteen minutes. If Yvonne didn't show up soon, the timing of the plan was going to be thrown off!

All at once the door flew open and Nancy found herself face-to-face with the publisher. "Nancy!" Yvonne exclaimed. "What are you doing here?" She gave her a sugar-coated smile.

Nancy smiled, too, just as falsely as Yvonne had. "I have great news," she said. "I've discovered who's to blame for the murder attempts!"

"Oh, how wonderful," Yvonne said. Nancy could tell from the tone of her voice that Yvonne didn't think she'd been found out. "Sit down." She ushered Nancy onto the black couch. "Tell me all about it." Yvonne took her customary seat behind her desk.

Nancy sat down coolly on the couch. "It was an interesting case," she began, "very cleverly planned in the criminal's mind. I almost didn't crack it! But in the end I was able to, thanks to my partners—Agatha Christie, Sir Arthur Conan Doyle, and all the other fabulous mystery writers whose books I've read over the years."

A strange expression crossed Yvonne's face. It took Nancy a moment to realize that the publisher was scared! And that's the proof, Nancy decided. *She knows I know the truth and she's frightened!*

Nancy hurried on. "Yes," she said, "I've gotten tons of ideas from books. And I've found that criminals sometimes get ideas from books, too."

Yvonne pursed her lips. "What does all this have to do with the problems at *Flash*?"

Nancy wasn't about to answer the publisher's question—at least not yet. She smiled and asked, "What mystery writers do you like to read, Yvonne? I've just discovered a new one who's very interesting to me. Ivan Green. Ever heard of him?"

But Nancy hadn't counted on what happened next. Suddenly she was staring into the gleaming barrel of a hand revolver—and Yvonne was smiling evilly at her from behind it.

Chapter

Sixteen

"Don't make a sound," Yvonne said smoothly, not lowering the polished revolver, "or your face is going to be such a mess even plastic surgery won't help."

"I won't make a peep," Nancy replied. She hoped Yvonne wasn't trigger-happy. Otherwise she was going to be a memory before Ned and Sondra even had a chance to try the toy gun trick.

"You're smart, Nancy Drew," Yvonne was saying. "Smarter than I counted on. I didn't think you'd catch on to my little game. Well, it doesn't make much difference now because, my young detective, you're not careful enough!"

Nancy glanced anxiously over her shoulder at the door. Where were Ned and Sondra? They should have been there already, plastic pistol blazing.

"By the way," Yvonne added cruelly, "someone left the door to the darkroom open. I made sure it was locked from the outside before I came in here."

Nancy sucked in her breath. Uh-oh. She was on her own. "What are you going to do with me?" she asked calmly.

"In just a moment, I'm going to let you join your friends," Yvonne told her gleefully. "Then I will simply dispose of you all. But before I do, I'd like to know how you guessed my secret. I thought I'd created the perfect crime."

"Even the best-planned crimes have flaws," Nancy said. "Yours had a few. The most important one was that you lied to me."

"That's only a flaw if I did it badly," Yvonne cut in, "and I obviously did, since you found out the truth. Which lie are you talking about?" she asked.

"The first day I met you," Nancy continued, stalling for time, "you made a big deal about putting down mystery novels. Then Mick happened to mention that you loved them and had even written a few. I asked myself why you would lie about that to me. What did you have to hide? Then I remembered the copy of *Deadly Potion, Deadly Bite* that I'd seen in Mick's office just after the tarantula appeared in your desk."

"You were *supposed* to remember it,"

Yvonne commented sourly. "I planted it there to make Mick look guilty to you. I even stole one of his buttons, to make it absolutely clear."

"Right, but I realized later that the author, Ivan Green, was *you.*"

"I see," Yvonne said. "Then it wasn't a flaw in my planning. It was just a silly coincidence—Mick mentioning that I wrote mysteries."

"Silly coincidences are a detective's best friends," Nancy said seriously. "I've rarely solved a mystery without one. But you did make one mistake. When I felt your pulse after you 'fainted' the day the gunman 'broke into' *Flash,* it was racing. So your body tipped me off to another lie—you weren't really unconscious."

"You're thorough," Yvonne said disdainfully, "but clearly not thorough enough." She glanced down at her gun with a satisfied smile.

She's so sure of herself, Nancy thought. She studied Yvonne's face. I've got to get a full confession, she told herself. She needed undeniable evidence—just in case she managed to get out of this situation alive. The tape was running inside her bag. All she had to do was get Yvonne talking.

"I have a few questions, too," Nancy said after a moment. "How did you pull off the 'shooting' in your office? There's no way you could have shot the gun, planted it in Mick's office, and gotten back to your own office in the few seconds it took for us to run to your aid."

"It *was* a rather ingenious scheme, if I do say

so myself," Yvonne bragged. "I shot the bullet into the wall on Thursday, the night before the incident."

"That's right," Nancy said, suddenly understanding. "I saw your signature in the security guard's book when I came in to *Flash* on Saturday. That explains why the bullet was so far off the mark. You weren't aiming at any specific target! I figured no one was such a bad shot!"

"Very good," Yvonne said condescendingly. "Anyway, as you can guess, I also planted a gun in Mick's desk that night. Then on Friday, I used a second gun to get everyone's attention. I just shot out the window. Then I took it home with me since I knew you'd search my office. And I counted on your searching Mick's, too."

"Well, things almost turned out just the way you wanted," Nancy responded. "And now I've got one more question. Where does David fit into all this?"

"David?" Yvonne smirked. "That wimp? He's too stupid to pull off something like this. I was just using him to get to the top people at MediaCorp. I did it all, Nancy Drew, with no help from anyone!"

Well, I've got the confession, Nancy thought. Now if I can just get it and myself out of here. . . . But Yvonne was already standing up, holding a length of rope she'd obviously stashed in one of her desk drawers. Grinning nastily, she walked toward Nancy. Without taking either her eyes or her gun off the girl, she reached into Nancy's shoulder bag and removed the tape recorder.

"An old trick," Yvonne said, triumphantly flicking off the record button and ejecting the cassette. "This one's been used by mystery writers for a long time, too. Oh, well. I don't care if the confession's on tape—as long as *I've* got the tape."

Nancy swallowed hard. She hated being outsmarted.

Yvonne pocketed the tape and nudged Nancy's cheek with the gun. "Get moving, Detective. You've got a hot date—very hot, believe me."

Nancy didn't know what Yvonne was talking about, but she stood up and allowed Yvonne to direct her out of the office and toward the darkroom. Then the publisher reached into her pocket and handed Nancy the keys to the door. "Open it," she said. Nancy unlocked the door and Yvonne shoved her inside.

"Nancy!" Ned and Sondra shouted at once.

"Hi, guys. I think we messed up," Nancy said.

"Are you all right?" Ned cried. "If she's hurt you—"

"I'm fine," Nancy assured him. "Besides, there's nothing you can do to her, so you might as well not make idle threats."

"Smart girl," Yvonne said, obviously enjoying her power. "Okay, Nancy, you're about to become my assistant. I want you to tie up your friends. This gun will be trained on you while you work, so no funny stuff. If the knots aren't good and strong, the gun goes off. Got it?"

"Yes," Nancy muttered.

Yvonne handed Nancy the rope, and the young detective got to work tying Ned's hands behind his back. Yvonne watched over her shoulder, giving her directions and ordering her to pull tighter at every step. Nancy did her best to put a little slack into the knot, but when she was finished she had to admit that the knot wouldn't be easy to untie.

Nancy was forced to tie Ned's feet and Sondra's hands and feet in the same way. After that, Yvonne tied Nancy's herself. "Well," she said, once she was finished, "I hate to spoil the party, so I'll leave. But first I've got to fix you kids some refreshments."

Yvonne walked over to the cabinet near the darkroom sink where the chemicals were stored and pulled out a few bottles. She opened them and dumped the chemicals into a large bowl, mixing up a vile brew.

"With all the chemicals stored in darkrooms," Yvonne said nonchalantly, "fires start so easily." She sloshed the mixture along the floor, leaving a large puddle in front of the door. "This stuff should light up like desert brush in the dry season."

Yvonne took the tape with her confession on it and deftly deposited it on the worktable. "I can't think of anything nicer to do with this than start a bonfire," she said. She produced a book of matches from her pocket and lit one. "All right, my friends, don't get too hot under the collar."

Yvonne walked to the door and stepped just outside it. Then she pitched the match into the puddle of chemicals. They went up in a whoosh of flame. Yvonne slammed the door shut, and Nancy heard her lock it from the outside. The fire began to spread quickly.

Nancy tugged at the ropes that bound her hands. No use—Yvonne had done a professional job. "Ned, Sondra," she cried, "can either of you pull free of your ropes? It's our only chance."

"You kidding me?" Ned asked. "Houdini couldn't get out of these."

"Or these," Sondra called.

"Then that's it," Nancy said finally. "We're trapped!" Slowly the fire inched closer to the three teenagers.

Chapter

Seventeen

"WHAT ARE WE going to *do?*" Sondra cried, dangerously close to hysteria.

"Not sit here and burn up, that's for sure," Nancy replied. But as if to taunt her, the flames licked her toes. Nancy pulled her legs up to her chest.

"Calm down," Ned told Sondra. "Nancy's gotten out of worse situations than this."

"Well, what *are* you going to do?" Sondra whispered fearfully.

But Nancy didn't answer. She was too busy thinking. She knew that somehow she had to get free of the ropes that tied her hands and feet. Otherwise, all three of them were going to be burned crisper than a batch of overdone French fries. But how?

Ned had mentioned Houdini, the great escape artist. He'd been able to get out of complicated knots, metal chains, locked chests—sometimes while submerged in a tank of water! Of course, legend had it that Houdini had been killed when one of his tricks had failed—but that was after thousands of successful escapes. *Come on, Houdini, help us out!* Nancy prayed.

Suddenly Nancy realized the answer! Houdini had sometimes untied ropes with his teeth. Nancy had never done it before, but she was about to try!

"Sondra, Ned," Nancy shouted, "I've got it! Sondra, twist around so that your hands are facing me." Sondra did so, while Nancy scooted toward her. Meanwhile, the darkroom was growing hotter by the millisecond.

Nancy was so close to Sondra that she could smell her perfume over the scent of burning chemicals. With one more push, she had reached her, her face shoved up against the stylist's bound hands.

Immediately Nancy began to chew the knots with her teeth.

"Ow," Sondra shrieked.

Nancy spit the rope out of her mouth. "Did I bite you? I'm sorry."

"No," Sondra said, terrified. "It's the flames—they're getting closer!"

"Hurry, Nancy," Ned cried. "I'm about to pass out from the fumes!"

Nancy redoubled her efforts. Suddenly she felt the ropes loosen!

"Nancy," Sondra screamed, "they're coming undone! We're going to get out of here!"

Nancy gave one last jerk at the ropes which held Sondra. "Shake your arms," she cried. "Shake hard! Get those ropes off before the fire reaches us!"

Sondra pumped her hands frantically up and down, maneuvering as best she could with her arms pinned awkwardly behind her back. And then, all at once, she was free!

She turned to Nancy, and in a few moments Nancy felt the ropes falling off her hands.

"Sondra, work on your feet!" exclaimed Nancy. "I'll get Ned's hands!" Nancy crawled over to her boyfriend. In just a few more minutes the three teenagers were on their feet.

Sondra stared dismally around the room. The puddles of chemicals were burning brightly. Here and there stacks of photos and paper had caught on fire. "Now what?" she said. Flames danced in front of the door.

"Nancy," Ned cried, "the only exit is blocked! This is a darkroom. There aren't any windows."

"I'm not sure how we're going to get out of here," she said, "but I do know how we can stall for time!"

Nancy ran to the sink and filled a plastic bucket. She dashed the water against one flaming wall. But by the time she'd refilled the bucket, the fire was raging once again.

Suddenly Sondra sank to the floor in a dead faint.

"It's the smoke!" Nancy cried. "It can kill you faster than the flames themselves."

At that moment one of the walls collapsed in a shower of sparkling embers. Nancy could see something shining in the room beyond.

"That's it!" Nancy cried. "Look, Ned! It's an escape route, made by the fire."

Ned looked at the flaming opening in the wall. "Uh, one small problem, Nancy," he said. "I don't see how we're going to get through that hole alive!"

"Start bailing, Nickerson," Nancy ordered, tossing Ned a bucket. Together they dumped water on the fiery wall at a frantic pace. They managed to lessen the intensity of the flames, but not to put them out completely.

"This is the best we're going to do," Nancy told Ned. "Get Sondra and yourself out of here!"

"What about you, Nancy?"

"I've got to find that tape with Yvonne's confession. Without it, we're just three careless teenagers in a darkroom, playing with chemicals we don't know anything about. No jury in the world would take our word about this 'accident' against Yvonne's, believe me." Nancy gave her boyfriend a push. "Go on. I'm not intending to let myself go up in a puff of smoke!"

Ned planted a kiss on Nancy's soot-smudged cheek. "I love you," he said. Then he picked Sondra up and ran with her across the charred floor. Soon he and Sondra had disappeared through the glowing wall.

Meanwhile, Nancy was scouring the worktable for the tape. When she saw it, it was inches away from the fire, about to turn into a burnt memory itself. She grabbed it. If the heat hadn't damaged it too much, it meant she had Yvonne right where she wanted her, and ready for a good long jail term.

Nancy turned back to her escape route. She took a deep breath. Then, braving the flames that still licked at the charred hole, she scrambled through.

As Nancy emerged from the flaming darkroom, Ned ran to her and hugged her to him. "Thank heavens you're safe," he said, breathing heavily. "I've already called the fire department. Oh, Nancy, I don't know what I would have done if I'd lost you!"

All at once the tension and terror of the past few hours hit Nancy. She felt weak. All she wanted was a pair of strong arms around her, holding her. The anger and pain she'd been holding inside for the last few days dissolved into nothing. She sank gratefully against Ned's chest. "It's over," she said at last. Then she pulled away, looking frantically around the room. "Is Sondra all right?"

"She's fine," Ned whispered. "We're all fine, thanks to you."

Nancy smiled into Ned's dark, tender eyes. "Thank you, too, Ned. You kept a cool head in there." She sighed. "Um, Ned, I'd love to stay with you like this, but the office is on fire, you know."

Ned laughed. "I think maybe we'd better get out of here."

"I think maybe you're right!"

The two teenagers hurried out of the office, their arms wrapped around each other tenderly. They found Sondra in the lobby, waiting nervously by the elevators. As they stepped into the cool Chicago evening, they heard the musical wail of fire engines.

Chapter

Eighteen

"Mmm," Nancy purred with satisfaction as she soaked up the rays of the early spring sun. "There's nothing like a long weekend at the beach." She smiled happily and gazed across the serene blue waters of Fox Lake.

Ned laughed and reached out to squeeze Nancy's hand. "You know, that whole ridiculous fight never would have happened if you'd only been this enthusiastic about the vacation from the beginning!"

"What can I say?" Nancy asked. "I'm a workaholic when it comes to solving mysteries. I know it's a little crazy, but, as the saying goes, either love me or leave me."

Ned inched closer to Nancy and slipped his arm around her shoulders. "No way! Now that I've got you back, I'm hanging on to you. Even if I have to put up with your obsession with detective work."

Nancy laughed. She knew it was partly her passion for adventure and her desire to pursue a challenge that made Ned love her, in spite of the difficulties.

Ned stared seriously into Nancy's eyes. "I swear," he said, "leaving you behind in that burning darkroom was the hardest thing I've done in my life!"

"Harder than being tackled by those huge defensive linemen from Notre Dame during that last game?" Nancy teased.

"Much!" Ned said seriously, then added, "I always knew I loved you, Nancy, but now I really know how much."

"Well, I certainly learned *my* lesson," Nancy said. "If I want you to understand how much *I* love *you*, I've got to show it." She leaned over and brushed her lips lightly against Ned's. "Like this," she said softly. "And there's no time like the present to start."

Ned laughed. "Hey, make sure my parents don't see us. They'll get embarrassed."

Nancy giggled. "I will, too."

"Anyway," Ned said, returning Nancy's kiss, "I'm just glad we're finally here together and that everything's back to normal at *Flash*—or back to whatever passes for normal there." He stared up at the high blue sky.

"Yeah, they are kind of a crazy bunch," Nancy agreed. "But you know, I actually ended up getting kind of fond of them."

"Yeah, me, too," Ned said, lazily rubbing his hand up and down Nancy's arm.

"I'll say!" Nancy exclaimed. "You got a little carried away with one of them."

"Oh no, we don't have to go through the thing about Sondra again, do we?" Ned asked with a laugh. "I told you, we only kissed each other once."

"And that was one time too many! What was it like, anyway?"

"Weird, actually," Ned said, "to be kissing anyone other than you."

"Did she kiss better than I do?" Nancy asked.

"I'm not sure," Ned teased. "Pucker up and I'll do a comparison test."

Nancy laughed and pulled Ned into a playful embrace, meeting his tender lips with her own. It felt good to be close to him, sharing jokes and sharing love. She'd missed that so much over the past two weeks.

Finally, the couple broke apart. "You're better," Ned told Nancy. "Much better!"

"Smart answer, Ned," Nancy teased. She really couldn't be too mad at Ned about Sondra. Nothing much had happened, as it turned out. She figured that both she and Ned had learned a lot from the experience. For one thing, they had learned how much they belonged together. And for another, they'd learned that even though a little fling wasn't the most horrible thing in the world, it was best kept short and sweet.

"So what do you think will happen to all those people over at *Flash?*" Ned asked. He ran his hand gently through Nancy's silky hair.

"Well, I figure that Yvonne will get a good long jail sentence. After all, she did try to kill Mick at the Maggie Awards, and there were several thousand witnesses, plus nationwide television coverage!"

"I've got to hand it to Yvonne—when she does something, she does it in a big way."

"Yeah, well, that's Yvonne. She likes to make a splash," Nancy commented. "She'll probably have half the prison eating out of her hand by her second week there. Of course, she's blown her career. She's going to have to sell her part of *Flash* to Mick, and I'm sure no one will ever hire her again."

"But she'll have plenty of time to write while she's in jail," Ned said thoughtfully, "which is what she really enjoyed doing anyway."

"And the market for true crime stories is getting bigger and bigger," Nancy said with a smile. "I can just see her writing a best seller called *I Made a Killing in the Magazine Business.*"

"Well, she certainly has an imagination," Ned agreed. "It'll probably be a great book!"

"Anyway, I'm glad Mick's going to get the chance to run *Flash* his own way. He's already given MediaCorp a definite buzz-off signal and he told me he's going to try and make the magazine a more pleasant place to work."

"Getting rid of Yvonne will do wonders as far as that's concerned," Ned commented.

"And I hear that David sent in his resignation," Nancy told Ned. "I think he was just working at *Flash* because Yvonne was there."

"Yeah," Ned agreed. "He may have acted like a big slug around everyone else, but I think he actually loved Yvonne!"

"It must have been terrible for him to find out she was only interested in him for his connections with MediaCorp," Nancy said.

"Is he going back to the *Law Review?*" Ned asked.

"Yup. It's a good job. And Mick will get an editor in chief who's easier to work with. He deserves that. He's dedicated to *Flash,* and he's got a lot of creative ideas. With the Maggie award behind him, he's going to be a fabulous success."

"Creative ideas, huh?" Ned said. "For instance, a cover story on America's hottest girl detective?"

Nancy sighed, drawing patterns in the sand with her foot. "That's my one regret—that I had to turn down the article Mick wanted to do about me. But if I'd accepted, half the country would have found out who I was. It would have made it impossible to find a believable cover for any future cases."

"Right," Ned said. "Fame and sleuthing mix like oil and vinegar. Or like Mick and Yvonne!"

"Anyhow," Nancy continued, resting her

head on Ned's shoulder, "I wasn't about to blow my whole career as a detective for one week in the spotlight."

She and Ned sat silently for a moment, absorbing the peace of the lake and the warmth of each other's company. The trees around the glistening water swayed in the kiss-soft breeze.

"Anyway, I went back to *Flash* after it was all over, and things had already changed," Nancy commented. "Suddenly everyone was crazy about me."

"I'm sure it felt good to straighten things out with the *Flash* staff, right?"

"Sure," Nancy said, smiling happily at Ned. "Lots of those guys were really nice. I guess I can't blame them for being suspicious of me."

"I hear the damage to the offices wasn't too bad," Ned said.

"Yeah, only the darkroom and one wall of Mick's office were badly damaged. Once they air the place out, make a few repairs, and find a new editor, *Flash* is going to be better than ever."

"That's good," Ned said, sliding his arm around Nancy's waist.

"Hey," Nancy said suddenly, "you know, I'm supposed to meet Sondra for dinner next Wednesday. She's taking me to her favorite Italian restaurant."

"You're kidding!" Ned exclaimed. "I thought she made you want to commit murder every time you saw her!"

Nancy laughed. "I guess she did at first, but it

didn't have anything to do with Sondra herself. Now that I know a little more about her, I think we're going to be friends. At the beginning, I was just jealous."

"Then you admit it!"

"Sure," Nancy said. "And I'm not proud of it. But I think I have that under control now. Being stuck in that burning room with her definitely brought us closer. She was pretty brave, and I have to respect her for that. I mean, most people would have flipped out in that situation."

"Except for you," Ned pointed out.

"Yeah, but I've been stuck in dangerous places before," Nancy said with a giggle, "so I've had some practice."

Ned slipped his other arm around her and gave her a gentle hug. "Well, try not to do too much more practicing. I love you. I don't want you getting hurt, or even cutting it as close as you did in that darkroom." He kissed her on each cheek before finding her lips.

"Okay," Nancy murmured, "I'll try to stay out of trouble, because I love you, too, Ned."

But the young detective had crossed her fingers behind her boyfriend's back. I'll try, she thought, until the next mystery comes along.

Nancy's next case:

When Nancy arrives in Fort Lauderdale for spring break, all she expects is a good time and a tan. But that's before a hit-and-run driver puts her friend Kim in the hospital.

This is no accident. Someone is trying to keep Kim from talking. But what is she hiding? Nancy finds suspects everywhere. When her top suspect is murdered, Nancy knows she's getting close—maybe too close—to the truth.

Nancy finds herself surrounded by gorgeous guys and deadly intrigue. Is she in over her head?

Find out in *HIT AND RUN HOLIDAY,* Case #5 in *The Nancy Drew Files™*.